DRAGON MAID

HIGHLAND FANTASY ROMANCE

ANN GIMPEL

CONTENTS

DRAGON MAID

~

by Ann Gimpel
Highland Fantasy Romance
Dragon Lore, Book Three

Tumble off reality's edge into myth, magic, and Celtic dragon shifters.

BOOK DESCRIPTION, DRAGON MAID

Books in the Dragon Lore Series:
Highland Secrets
To Love a Highland Dragon
Dragon Maid
Dragon's Dare

When pressed, Jonathan Shea admits magic runs through his blood, but he's always been ambivalent about it—until a dragon and her mage show up in the Scottish Highlands, and then all bets are off. Jonathan's charmed and captivated by the dragon—a creature fresh out of myth and legend—but the woman bonded to the dragon is incredible.

Freshly arrived from a much earlier time, Britta feels awkward, out of place. The first person she lays eyes on is Jonathan. There's something about him. She can't quite pinpoint it, but he has way more magic than he lets on. Magic aside, for the first time ever, she questions the wisdom of remaining a maid. If she doesn't make up her mind damned fast, though, her choices will fritter away. Beset from every side, she's never needed her magical ability more.

this all-out war and the part they play in the battle and the universe that has been created.

Dragon Maid is the second book in the Dragon Lore series. I loved book 1 and was looking forward to reading this one. Ann Gimpel is an amazing author who manages to captivate her readers with her stories. This book picked up right where we left off in book one. Lachlan, Kheladin and Maggie are still fighting to destroy the Morrigan.

This book picks up right where the previous installment left off and hurls readers into a world of magic, action-packed scenes, a captivating romance, and a race to save the world with the help of a dragon and Mage from the past. From the first page to the last this is a read that draws you in, even if the mythos is confusing at times, and leaves you anticipating the next installment after the revelations revealed here.

Dragon Maid was such a captivating continuation of the *Dragon Lore* series. Gimpel weaves a story full of all the things I love most: passion, adventure, intrigue, and smexy times with a most delicious alpha male. The Book Chick

I really like these books and am constantly surprised by the detail that goes into this series. The world building is excellent and the storyline is an incredible one that just keeps building. Strong characters make this book truly stand out and the level of emotion portrayed is never sickly sweet but feels so realistic.

and endearing. I'm usually one who can see what's coming next, however Ann has really surprised me with her twists and turns. This book was pure heaven to read, had me hooked from the start.

To Love a Highland Dragon was a mix of two of my favorite fictions elements—hunky Highlanders and shapeshifters, specifically dragon shifters. I absolutely adored Lachlan, Maggie, and the dragon, Kheladin.

I'm not big on time travel books, but this one I loved. It was awesome to read about the different levels of love between the characters.

I've never read a dragon shifter book before, and didn't know if I would like it, but this is one of those stories that carries you on a wave so wonderful you just don't want to get off.

*L*achlan bent his head and kissed Maggie. She arched against him, opening her mouth, and he tightened his hold on her.

Maybe leaving her with her grandmother, even for the short time it would take him to do what he needed, wasn't the best idea. He tangled his hands in the blonde hair streaming down her back and kissed her more thoroughly, teasing her tongue with his.

Someone tapped his shoulder.

Mary Elma, Maggie's grandmother—and the most powerful witch alive—cleared her throat. She didn't say anything. She didn't have to. They had a plan, and a damned good one, but he needed to do his part.

He dragged his mouth from Maggie's and gazed fondly at her. "Lassie. Open your eyes."

She did, her brilliant blue eyes twinkling with amusement. "If you're going to let Gran push you around from the get-go, there'll be no hope for us. I heard her too." She shot a sidelong glance at Mary Elma. "I chose to ignore her."

"*Tsk.* No respect." But Mary Elma was smiling. It was obvious she loved her granddaughter dearly and was willing to overlook a lot. Long dark hair fell almost to her waist around her wraith-thin body. Dressed in black as usual, her dark eyes shone warmly.

Lachlan laid a hand on Maggie's cheek. "I willna be gone long. And ye really do need to work on your magic."

Maggie rolled her eyes. "I suppose a crash course is long overdue, especially given I had zero interest in anything witchy until I met you."

"What a gross understatement!" Mary Elma pursed her lips. "The enormous infusion of magic Mauvreen and I force-fed you needs to be shaped and honed. You could actually do damage without more knowledge."

"Your gran speaks true." Lachlan arranged a stray strand of hair behind Maggie's ear. "I felt great power within you, even afore your gran and Mauvreen added to it. Ye're truly a force to be reckoned with now." The miracle of her in his arms was so enticing, he'd never leave if he couldn't put some distance between them. Lachlan brushed a knuckle over Maggie's full lips and stepped away from her.

Maggie looked from him to Mary Elma. "What if the *force to be reckoned with* wants her brand new husband to stay awhile longer?"

"Och, mo croi, I do love you. We've had such a wee bit of time together, 'tisn't easy to leave you, even for a span of a few hours."

Mary Elma made shooing motions with her hands. "Never fear, dragon shifter, I'll take good care of your bride."

"I know ye will. Kheladin and I will be back verra soon. I suppose he's still in the yard with Mauvreen."

"That would be a solid deduction," Mary Elma said wryly. "I'd never have guessed a dragon would be such a sucker for attention."

Lachlan bristled. "Kheladin is far from a pushover. He recognizes Mauvreen's adulation as genuine. 'Twas a time when humans worshiped dragons, and he misses it."

It was amazingly difficult to leave Maggie's presence, but Lachlan forced himself to turn and walk out the door of Mauvreen's house. Swathed in spells, it appeared to be a charming, white-washed cottage to passersby, but it was actually an old, multi-story stone manse, sitting just north of Fort William deep in the Scottish Highlands.

Lachlan located his dragon and Mauvreen chatting up a storm. Steam billowed from the copper-colored dragon's nostrils, and he gestured with his forelegs when he talked. Mauvreen nodded enthusiastically, apparently agreeing with whatever pearls of wisdom Kheladin dispensed.

She waved eagerly when she noticed Lachlan. He strode down her front steps and across the yard, which was shrouded in wardings and *don't look here* spells.

Kheladin blew steam at him. "I was wondering if we were ever going to leave," the dragon said.

"Yes," Mauvreen seconded. "Here we were thinking maybe you'd changed your mind about visiting the Celts."

Lachlan shrugged. Truth be told, he was of two minds because he saw their trip as a fool's errand. Nevertheless, he had to try to secure the Celtic gods' assistance. The Morrigan, also known as the Battle Crow, was one of their own—and she was out of control. By rights, they should be the ones to manage her outrageous behavior. Like all Celts, she was immortal, which further complicated matters.

Kheladin eyed him shrewdly. He and Lachlan were bondmates. Over the hundreds of years they'd been a pair, they'd gotten to know one another eerily well. "We must do this thing," he rumbled and belched a gout of fire.

"I ken as much, but it doesna mean I believe it a wise course of action."

Kheladin hunkered until he could lay a taloned forefoot on Lachlan's shoulder. "Rhukon and his dragon, Malik, nearly bested us —again. Connor and his dragon, Preki, aren't as big a problem, but the Morrigan controls them too. If it werena enough that they ensorcelled us for over three hundred years, they just dragged us back to the fifteen hundreds to try to keep you away from Maggie."

Lachlan nodded tiredly. "I havena forgotten. If it wasna for you and your quick thinking, we'd still be stuck hundreds of years in the past."

Leaving the Morrigan free to spread chaos and poison throughout time.

Kheladin twisted his long stalk of a neck and looked pointedly at the spot between his wings. Lachlan drew magic and vaulted into place.

"Is the invitation to bring my coven to your cave still open?" Mauvreen asked, hope shining from her amber eyes.

"Of course. I'll join you there once Lachlan and I return from the Isle of Skye." The dragon spread his wings.

"Thanks. See you soon." Mauvreen winked. "We can finish our conversation then."

"Ye'll have to remind me where we left off," the dragon called.

"Glad to." Mauvreen turned and walked toward the house, her spiky red curls bouncing around her well-rounded form.

"I'd love to fly with you," Lachlan told the dragon, "but doona ye think we should use magic to travel?"

"I miss the time we came from," Kheladin grumbled.

"Aye, I understand, yet we willna accomplish anything if some modern do-gooder sees us and tries to shoot us out of the sky."

Kheladin folded his wings. "I would kill them."

"And then we would be in even deeper trouble. We havena spent long in this era. 'Twould be wise for us to blend in as best we can." Lachlan summoned a traveling spell. He visualized the standing stone circle on the Isle of Skye and took them there. He wasn't certain he'd find any of the Celts, but the stones held a great deal of ancient power. If the Celts were elsewhere, perhaps one would notice him waiting and deign to come.

He cast invisibility about himself and his dragon before they emerged from his spell. No point in scaring the hell out of tourists who might be visiting the standing stones. He had ways of getting rid of them, but he couldn't do it from a distance.

He smelled the salt air before the sacred circle wavered into view.

Deserted.

Lady luck was with him. He glanced at a clear blue sky and imagined a thundercloud or two. A few drops pattered down, settling into a steady downpour. Nothing like a little rain to discourage stray visitors. Kheladin dug into the sand, his jaws parted in his approximation of a grin. Lachlan jumped down, using magic to soften his landing. The dragon was large enough, falling from his back would be like tumbling off a six foot precipice.

Lachlan settled in to wait, creating a minor spell to divert rain from the top of his head.

"'Tis good to see you happy." Kheladin nudged him with his snout.

"Aye. Maggie is everything my dreams were made of." Lachlan twisted so he looked Kheladin in the eye. "She makes up for having to live in the midst of concrete, asphalt, toxic water, and poisoned air."

The dragon snorted steam. "She said she'd be willing to come back to the fifteen or sixteen hundreds with us, for at least part of the time."

"Aye, that she did." Lachlan leaned against Kheladin's warm scales and lapsed into thought. Maggie was his destiny. Their pairing was foretold eons ago and held enough magic to save the world from the Morrigan and her henchmen. It was why Rhukon expended so much effort trying to keep him and Maggie apart.

Rhukon had even gone so far as to separate Maggie from the dream world, intent on capturing her. Thank the goddess, her magic was potent enough to stymie him. She'd been frantic, and her efforts fueled by fear, but it was hard to argue with success.

In spite of Rhukon, the Morrigan, and the red wyvern, the pull of destiny had been impossible to deny. Lachlan found Maggie, anyway. Or she found him. That they were together infuriated the Morrigan. She upped the ante and escalated from an annoyance to an outright menace. Even though Mary Elma cautioned him the Celtic gods were unlikely to help—something Lachlan already knew—both of them saw today's journey as necessary.

Light leached from the long, summer's day. Lachlan was getting ready to tell Kheladin it was high time they left. If the Celts knew he stood in their sacred circle, they apparently weren't going to acknowledge him. He could force the issue by calling for them directly, but didn't wish to anger them. The air shimmered off to one side. Lachlan blinked. When his vision cleared, Ceridwen, Gwydion, and Arawn stood in a semicircle, glowering.

Ceridwen, goddess of the world, crossed her arms over her chest. Long black hair, shot with silver, cascaded down her robed body. "We know what ye want," she said without preamble, and certainly without so much as a greeting to preface her stark words.

"Aye." Gwydion, master enchanter and warrior magician, blew out a tired sounding sigh. Blond hair wafted about him, dampening quickly from the rain. He jabbed a richly carved wooden staff into the ground for emphasis. "'Tisn't as if ye havena asked afore."

Lachlan focused his gaze on Arawn, god of the dead. Today his midnight-dark hair was unbound and his dark eyes solemn.

"Ye must figure this problem out on your own," the god of the underworld said.

Ceridwen shook her head. Lightning flashed next to her, so Lachlan understood she was furious. "We almost dinna come."

"Aye," Arawn added. "The reason ye waited for hours is because we argued about it."

"'Twas only my fondness for you that prevailed," Gwydion muttered. "Doona push me, dragon shifter. I wouldna like to think ye'd take advantage of my good nature."

"But I havena even opened my mouth as yet," Lachlan protested.

"Ye doona have to," Ceridwen snapped. "We see what is within your mind."

Kheladin got to his feet and turned to face the gods. "The Morrigan is one of you," he said flatly. "When a dragon misbehaves, we address it among ourselves. We doona foist the task off onto another race."

Lachlan winced. Kheladin's words were true, but he was afraid they'd make things worse.

"Humph." Gwydion pounded his staff into the ground again. "'Tisn't as if the Morrigan has done anything worse than her usual."

Arawn nodded agreement. "If anything, she may have been a wee bit better here of late."

"Only because there are no wars to feed her blood lust," Ceridwen growled. "Not big ones, anyway." She walked to Lachlan and thumped him in the chest with an index finger. "Rhukon and Connor are dragon shifter mages—just like you. Malik and Preki are dragons—just like Kheladin. We," she spread her arms to encompass Arawn and Gwydion, "have discussed this thoroughly. We see them as *your* problem."

Lachlan opened his mouth to protest, to tell them the Morrigan made Rhukon, Connor, and their dragons a much bigger problem than they'd be without her magic powering theirs. He considered reminding them of their duty to protect humankind.

Kheladin spoke deep within his mind. *"Doona argue. It willna help."*

Ceridwen waited. She glanced from Lachlan to Kheladin and back. "Much better," she said and shoved sodden hair behind her shoulders. "Now, we'll hear no more of this."

Gwydion trotted to Lachlan's side and clapped him on the back. "There's a good lad. Come visit when ye doona want something." His broad-shouldered form took on an insubstantial air. Moments later, the Celtic gods were gone.

"There's a good lad?" Lachlan snarled. He pounded a fist into the nearest stone and yelped.

Kheladin blasted fire toward the skies, a sure sign he was

seriously displeased. "The only way this could've gone worse," he growled, "would've been if they'd challenged us to a battle."

Lachlan knew better. He walked to the dragon's side. "Nay," he said. "Had they been truly bent on harming us, they'd have dissolved our bond."

CHAPTER 1

few hours later

Kheladin sat back on his haunches, his multi-chambered dragon heart bursting with delight. He breathed a gout of steam, and it drifted lazily upward. Crossing his forelegs over the copper scales cascading down his chest, he opened his jaws in a toothy grin.

The dragon gazed about his cave located deep beneath Inverness. It teemed with witches. This was the first time he'd entertained anyone except Lachlan or the Celtic gods, and his human bondmate scarcely counted because—until very recently—they'd been stuck shuttling between Lachlan's human body and his dragon one.

Kheladin's grin broadened. What a stroke of fortune when he stumbled on the arcane spell that allowed them to separate. Though he and Lachlan were still magically linked, they were no longer jammed into a single body. The freedom of his thoughts, without constant commentary from Lachlan, felt like a gift from the gods.

Mauvreen pushed her wild mop of red curls out of her face. Hair hung around her like a gown, falling to her waist. She was dressed in dark-colored breeks, much like a man would wear, and a fuzzy-looking green top with a black vest over it. Eyes the color of aged whiskey beamed at him.

She swept her arms wide. "Thanks for inviting us. Everyone's fascinated, simply fascinated, with you and your gold and gems, and well, just everything. Your storytelling's been great too." She walked a few steps from him and sank to the floor of his cave, joining a group of witches.

She looked back over a shoulder. "We're all here. You wanted me to let you know."

"Thank you." Kheladin secured his wards, grateful nothing wicked tried to sneak in, along with the group of witches.

He didn't count well. It wasn't a dragon gift, but at least thirty witches spread across the sandy floor of his cave. Maybe even forty or fifty. They'd been dribbling in for the past couple hours. Mage lights bobbed everywhere. What surprised him most was the number of males in the group. He'd always assumed most witches were women.

More steam, mingled with smoke, streamed from his open mouth. Kheladin assumed a lot of things, but many of them were no longer true. He shook himself from shoulders to tail tip. His scales rattled, filling the air with discordant chiming. What a shock it had been to waken in the early years of the twenty-first century after being ensorcelled with Lachlan for over three hundred years. The world had changed while they slumbered—and not for the better. He thought about the crowded streets of the city above them and grimaced. The sixteen hundreds' version of Inverness was a far more habitable place. At least then, he could appear aboveground. Not anymore.

He crooked a talon at Mauvreen. She pushed up from her place on the floor and strode to him. "What does my dragon desire?"

Fire joined smoke and steam, shooting high into the dark air above him. "I am not *your dragon*."

She waved a dismissive hand. "Don't be so touchy. I know you're bonded to Lachlan. It was just an endearment…sweetie. Speaking of Lachlan, will he be along soon?"

"I left him at your house in Fort William with Maggie and her grandmother. They'll show up when they choose."

"Could you pin it down a bit closer? I'm anxious to confer with Mary Elma."

"I'm not your servant to be ordered about." The dragon's whirling eyes spun faster in annoyance. What in the nine hells had happened to respect for ancient creatures? It was another aspect of modern life he didn't appreciate.

He started to chastise her, but swallowed the words. Not much point. Instead, he asked, "How many of your fellows are here?"

She narrowed her eyes in thought. "By my last count, fifty-three. Nearly the entire coven, except a handful who were out of town, else they'd be here too. How many other opportunities do you think we've gotten to lay eyes on a living, breathing dragon? It's not something any witch worth their salt would want to miss."

A male witch pressed forward, but stopped a respectful distance away.

Good! At least this human understands deference.

Kheladin studied him. The man was tall, about Lachlan's height, with broad shoulders fading to slender hips. Coal-black braids wove together in an intricate pattern that reminded Kheladin of early Celtic warriors. The braids lay close to the man's head and were gathered into a queue that spilled down his back. Arresting amber eyes radiated sharp intelligence. At the moment, they were hooded in concentration. He clasped his hands behind his back, obviously waiting.

'Tis just like the old times. He's giving me an opportunity to acknowledge him afore speaking.

The small concession pleased Kheladin. He inclined his head. "Your name, human."

Mauvreen whipped around. Apparently, she hadn't heard the

man take up a position behind her. "Go ahead, Johnny, speak up." She motioned with both hands.

The man tightened his jaw in what looked like barely constrained annoyance. "I understand you've known me since I was a child, but I still wish you wouldn't call me that." He took a few steps nearer Kheladin. "Thank you for giving me leave to address you, sir. My name is Jonathan James Shea." The faintest touch of an Irish lilt trod beneath the words.

The dragon inclined his head. "I am Kheladin."

The man's mouth twitched. "I know."

Curiosity burned. Dragons were long gone from this world. Unlike Lachlan, who'd been born in the early thirteen hundreds, the man standing before him was young, maybe only thirty or forty years. "I'm not surprised ye know about dragons, but how do ye know about me?"

Jonathan squared his shoulders. A rosy hue brightened tanned skin, setting off the sharp lines of his cheekbones and jaw. "I grew up steeped on dragon legends. When other lads put the fairytale books away, I kept reading them and just didn't tell anyone. Some of the more ancient scrolls my da kept noted many of your names."

Kheladin snorted, bathing Jonathan and Mauvreen in steam. "Ye're a man fully grown now. What do ye do other than keep fable books hidden beneath your bed?"

"I do not—" Jonathan broke off. He looked abashed, and the color in his face deepened. "You're teasing."

"Aye, but I would still like to know."

"I gave up reading fable books long since. I'm a software engineer. And a closet witch."

'Tis English, but it may as well be a foreign tongue. Best take them one at a time.

"Software engineer?"

Jonathan nodded. "That's right. Probably didn't make a bit of sense to you. I design programs that run in computers. Actually, I build gaming software for simulated war games. Kids love them. Grownups too."

"This cell phone is like a miniature computer," Mauvreen cut in helpfully. She drew a small, black oblong out of one of her pockets and waved it in the air.

"Aye." The dragon nodded his understanding. "I've seen them. 'Twould be hard not to since every person in Inverness seems to have one." Kheladin returned his attention to Jonathan. "What's inside the wee black box?"

"Um, I don't work on cell phones, but there are lots of different electronic parts and a miniature circuit board..." He creased his forehead into serious lines. "It's not important, not really."

"What is important?" Kheladin kept his spinning gaze focused on the man before him, this Jonathan Shea who was a software engineer and some special sort of witch.

Jonathan looked appraisingly at the dragon. "What I thought I heard, when you were talking to the group of us earlier, was that you and Lachlan can still share a body."

"Aye, we can—'tis how I know about all the cell phones in Inverness—but we're no longer forced to." Kheladin watched Jonathan, wondering why he'd highlighted that particular point.

"The best thing, then, would be for you to be in Lachlan's body, and I could bring you to my office—which is also my home—and show you about electronics and circuit boards." Jonathan grinned crookedly. "There's a saying: a picture is worth a thousand words."

"Even I know that one. Now, what did ye mean by *closet witch*? Is there a particular variety of witch? Do ye meet in closets?"

Mauvreen threw her head back and laughed. After a moment, Jonathan joined her. Anger surged. Fire roared from Kheladin's mouth. How dare these puny humans laugh at him?

Mauvreen got herself under control quickly. She bowed and then straightened. "We mean no offense. I'm certain if we got dumped in the fifteen or sixteen hundreds, there'd be many a turn of phrase we wouldn't understand. Johnny." She motioned with a fluttery hand. "Tell him what you have in mind."

He drew his arched, black brows together until they resembled raven's wings. "Our coven is a bit unusual because we have nearly as many men as women. Male witches are still not particularly well-accepted. Now if I were a Druid, it would be an entirely different affair since they're mostly men. At least now they are. In earlier times, the Celts were the only ones to give women close to equal rights."

"Ye doona have to tell me, laddie. I was there. I still doona understand the term *closet*."

"Sorry." Jonathan smiled, his teeth very white against his bronzed skin. "It just means I don't tell anyone outside the coven about my mystic side—or my magic."

Something about Jonathan's power puzzled Kheladin. The witch was muting it, but it was hard to tell how much. "Stand verra still," Kheladin instructed.

"Why?"

"I wish to test your power."

"H-how?"

"Afore ye are finished interrogating me, we could've been done. 'Tis a courtesy I asked instead of simply looking for myself." Kheladin reminded the witch of the enormous power differential between them.

"All right." Jonathan shut his eyes. It looked as if he were bracing for an onslaught.

Kheladin bit back a snort. "It willna hurt." He pushed his mind into the man before him, bypassing his wards easily, and drew back, amazed. Jonathan was still frozen in place. "Ye can move now."

"That's it?" Jonathan shook his head. "I didn't feel a thing."

The dragon did snort then. "And why would ye?" he inquired from behind a curtain of steam. "If I canna seek information without alerting humans to my presence within them, what good would my magic be?"

"Sorry. There's a lot I don't know."

"Good ye realize it." Kheladin looked from Jonathan to Mauvreen. It was obvious the man had no idea how much power he held. Compared with Mauvreen, he could move worlds. And if he was a witch, Kheladin was a Centaur. The dragon gazed about the assembled witches chatting in small groups. Were any of them other types of magic-wielders masquerading as witches? If so, did they hold anything akin to Jonathan's level of ability?

If they did, he and Lachlan could train them to help in the battles that were sure to come.

The black and red wyverns—Malik and Preki—and their mage bondmates—Rhukon and Connor—were still loose in the world, as was the Morrigan. From the looks of things, they were likely to remain so. He and Lachlan had had several narrow escapes, and Kheladin was certain the Morrigan wasn't anywhere close to backing down. He shut his scaled lids for a moment. Lachlan's mate, Maggie, wasn't immortal, which complicated matters greatly because they needed to keep her safe.

Mauvreen turned to face the assemblage. She used magic to project her voice. "Kheladin has been a great host. Let's help him set his cave to rights. It's the least we can do to thank him for inviting us."

"I'll help," a woman cried.

"Me too," another said.

"Yes, just tell us what to do," a third witch called out.

Kheladin puffed steam. Moving among them as they worked would be a good way to ascertain who had the most power. It might also afford a perfect opportunity to tell them about the dangers they faced—just to get them used to the idea.

"Excellent. Before you begin, would you like to know how my cave came to be littered with boulders?"

A rustling susurrus moved through the crowd. They surged closer, anxious to listen.

Kheladin took it as a good sign and began to talk. "Lachlan, a dragon shifter mage, is my bondmate. Not so long ago, he and I were forced to occupy a single form—his or mine. We'd just wakened after being ensorcelled for over three hundred years when he met Maggie Hibbins, a witch like all of you. Their mating was foretold, but it infuriated our enemies."

"Why?" someone cried.

"Was that why you were ensorcelled?" another witch asked.

The dragon paused, considering which details were needed. "Maggie and Lachlan are linked through a verra old prophecy. The simple version is their combined energy, once mated, will be enough to defeat our enemies and return Earth to its former glory. Of course," he preened, remembering his mating bite, "I was part of the mating too."

Mauvreen spun to face him and put her hands on her hips. "Not that I don't want to believe you, but Earth's pretty much on a one-way track to destruction. How could—?"

He puffed more steam to silence her and spoke sternly. "Ye are a witch. It means ye believe in magic. Prophecies are applied magic. Magic ye can see and feel and get your talons into. When ye canna believe in the wonder of it anymore, mayhap ye should rethink yourself."

She looked down. Kheladin read shame in her mind, but didn't soften his words by adding to them.

"It's one of the problems with being alive today." Jonathan spread his hands in front of him. "We live in an age that's antithetical to magic. Obviously, I wasn't there, but I'll bet it's a whole lot different than the time you came from. Everything is science-based now." He looked up, meeting, and holding the dragon's gaze. "Although when you explained applied magic, it sounded a lot like science to me." He shrugged. "Maybe it's just my mindset."

Few humans could tolerate a dragon's gaze. Fewer still sought it out. Kheladin was reluctantly impressed. "Come closer." He crooked a curved talon toward Jonathan. "Ye can explain *science* to me while the others clear rocks and debris from my cave floor."

He made shooing motions with both forelegs. "Go on, all of you. Get busy. I'll tell you more about Lachlan and me and the disorder in my cave later."

I can seek out those who may have strong magic another time. It doesna appear the witches are in any hurry to leave.

"You heard the dragon." Mauvreen bolted toward the group, obviously anxious to put distance between herself and the dragon who embarrassed her by pointing out her lapse of faith.

"I dinna mean to humiliate you." Kheladin used mind speech only she could hear.

She glanced over one shoulder and took her time answering. *"It was a shock having you peer into my innermost thoughts and pluck out what troubles me. In truth, I owe you a debt of thanks for making me examine what's uncomfortable."*

"You're welcome. If you wish to talk more later—"

"I'd like that." Mauvreen bent and picked up a rock, which she carted off to one side.

"Mauvreen. Over here." A witch with long, blonde hair beckoned. "If a few of us concentrate our magic, this won't take nearly as long."

Kheladin grinned to himself. He could've cleared the cave in minutes with his own magic, but it was heady having all these humans falling over themselves to help him. Almost like the old days. Perhaps once they got through the worst of things, and the black and red wyverns and the Morrigan had been soundly defeated, he'd float the idea of resurrecting shrines—hell, maybe even temples—to dragon worship.

He focused his gaze on Jonathan. The man didn't look away. "Step closer still. I doona bite." He chuckled, blowing steam. "Unless it's part of the mating ritual. Now, about this science…"

Jonathan strode next to Kheladin and craned his neck to glance up. "I thought it would be handy if we were looking at one another, but I'm not sure how to make it work."

"How about this?" Kheladin bent and extended a foreleg. "Hop on."

"Really?" Jonathan's eyes widened.

"I wouldna have offered in jest."

Jonathan positioned himself between Kheladin's front limbs and body. Once there, he stepped on the dragon's bent knees and levered himself up until he was seated on a foreleg. Jonathan swept his forthright gaze over Kheladin. "Perfect. Forgive me for staring, but you're incredible. I still can't believe this is really happening—"

"Science," Kheladin reminded him and straightened to his full height with the human balanced on his front leg.

"Oh yes, right. Well, the Scientific Revolution actually began during an era you likely remember. You'll recall Newton, Copernicus, Descartes, and Galileo, to name a few."

"Aye. They were regarded as charlatans."

"Why am I not surprised they weren't appreciated in their own time? In any event, by the seventeen and eighteen hundreds, which I guess you slept through, science was in full swing. If you couldn't prove something in a lab, it didn't exist. Talk about a death knell for magic and magic wielders. Somewhere around the sixteen-nineties, they started hanging witches in the States. On this side of the Atlantic, they burned them at the stake. I lost quite a few relatives—"

The air currents thickened. Magic. Strong magic that had nothing to do with the witches in his cave. The human sitting atop his foreleg stiffened. Apparently, he sensed it too. Kheladin bent forward, allowing Jonathan to scramble to the ground where he eyed the dragon.

"I've never felt anything quite like that. What is it?" He raised his hands to call power.

"I doona know. We will stand ready but not deploy defensive magic until we know what we face." He trumpeted. The sound rang off the cave's walls and echoed, amplifying itself. When it faded,

Kheladin spoke to everyone. "Something comes. Ready yourselves but doona loose your magic yet."

The oddness in the air intensified. It felt thick, syrupy, with a tinge of springtime. Kheladin chinked a hole in the warding he'd resurrected once the last witch was through. The minute he did, he knew what was outside his wards, but the answer was so fantastic, he had trouble believing it. Against all odds, another dragon shifter was close, one of the women.

Who had tracked him down? And why?

I willna have to wait long to find out.

"'Tis safe enough," he announced. "Return to your work. Another dragon will be here verra soon."

Another dragon, reverberated through the witches' ranks, along with *amazing, brilliant, incredible,* and *yesssss.*

Good to know we're still treasured.

"Drop your bloody wards, Kheladin. You recognized me. In the name of Dewi, let me in."

His wards.

Kheladin withdrew the magic powering them. *"Sorry. Done."*

Power raged through multihued air. When it stopped pulsating, an iridescent red dragon stood before him. Golden eyes whirled menacingly. Fire shot from her mouth. "What the bloody fuck? Why did ye hesitate once ye knew 'twas me?"

Kheladin slammed his wards shut and inclined his head. "I dinna realize 'twas you, Tarika. All I knew was another of us stood without. Besides, I havena seen you for over three hundred years. I thought ye'd gone to Fire Mountain with most of the rest of our kin."

"Humph." Tarika's gaze swept the cave. "Who are all these people?"

"Witches. And others. They like me."

"Pfft. Ye are so full of yourself." More fire, mixed with steam. "Let us take our human forms. I would lay eyes on Lachlan again."

"He's not here."

"What?" she screeched in a shower of sparks. "Ye broke the bond?"

"Aye and resurrected it in a superior form that allows us each the pleasure of our own bodies." He blew out a breath, aware the witches were fascinated and listening intently. "'Tis a verra long tale. I would start at the beginning."

Tarika blew smoke until cinders drifted around her. "Och, I recall that binding. Better for dragons." She shook her head, making her scales rattle. "I have no idea why it fell out of favor."

Kheladin shrugged to the accompaniment of more clanking scales. "I dinna know of it until I conferred with another First Born, like you, back in the fifteen hundreds—"

"Do ye have food here?" She broke in, talking over him.

"Nay. For sustenance, ye must leave my cave in human form. This era doesna recognize those like us."

"Fine."

The air turned molten gold, glistening and shimmery. When it cleared, Tarika's bondmate, Britta, stood before him, naked as the day she was born. Red-blonde hair shrouded her to her waist. Golden eyes glinted a challenge as she squared broad shoulders.

"Which direction might I find food? Tarika and I searched long for you, and I'm famished."

Jonathan stepped forward, eyes averted, color high on his cheeks. "Welcome. I'm Jonathan." He bowed slightly. "I'd be glad to help any way I can. If you're interested, I brought a couple sandwiches with me, and I'm sure some of the other witches didn't come empty-handed. We planned to be here for a while. Until Kheladin kicked us out, actually."

Britta eyed him speculatively. "A witch who knows his place. I prefer them that way. My name is Britta Kilkerran, Countess of Cumbria. Lead out." She made shooing motions with both hands. "If ye have mead to go with the food, I would take drink as well."

CHAPTER 2

Jonathan tried not to stare, but it was a losing battle. The woman—no, the dragon shifter—was the most perfect, the most alluring, creature he'd ever laid eyes on. Tall, with high, rounded breasts, a slender waist, and curvy hips, she looked like a goddess. Who knew? Maybe she was. The Celts had many deities. He fumbled with his rucksack and pulled out a turkey sandwich on rye bread, which he handed to her.

She yanked the wrappings aside, dropping them onto the floor while she stuffed food into her mouth, chewing and swallowing quickly. "Ye said there were two of these meat and bread things." Britta surveyed him, her golden eyes alight with interest.

"Yes, I did. If I give you both, I'll be hungry."

She shrugged. "Not my problem. Also, I requested mead."

Jonathan's lips twitched. He corralled the smile that wanted out. Britta was an imperious bitch, yet there was something so undeniably appealing about her straightforward nature, it was impossible to feel offended. "No mead. At least I don't have any. We could ask the other witches, or if we found you some clothes, we could go into the city and buy a proper meal, and as much to drink as you wanted."

She cocked her head to one side and popped the last bite of sandwich into her mouth. "I can go as I am. Shall we walk or use magic, witch?"

"Um, no, you can't go as you are. You'd be arrested."

She tilted her chin up. "Why? I can see where I might freeze to death, but who would give a jolly fuck whether I'm dressed or not?"

Before he could craft an explanation, Kheladin stalked over, trailed by three female witches stroking the scales on his lower body. "Lachlan kept a clothes chest against the far wall." He pointed with a talon. "I'm certain some of his shirts and tights would work, though there's little to be done by way of shoes."

Britta's gaze landed on a particularly large heap of gold jewelry and coins. "I could borrow a bit of money from your hoard, just a coin or two, and—"

Kheladin's eyes whirled faster, glittering dangerously. "I doona think so. Unless your First Born bondmate orders me."

"No need to disturb Tarika." Britta turned a brilliant smile on Jonathan and tapped his chest with her index finger. "He can buy me what I need." Magic shimmered around her. "Come close, witch. We're leaving."

Kheladin stumped to Britta's side. The counter spell he summoned to dampen her power sparkled, and multi-hued strands wrapped around her. Her lips curled in fury, and she raised her hands to call magic of her own.

"Not so fast," Kheladin snapped. "First, ye've forgotten ye need clothes. Second, Tarika was in an all-fired hurry to find me. Such a big hurry, ye went without food or rest. Why?"

Britta shook her head so hard, her hair danced about her body. She swept the heels of her hands down her cheeks, distorting her perfect features. "Och aye, whatever is wrong with me? Nay, I know the answer. The Morrigan is furious because Lachlan triumphed over the black and red wyverns, and their dragon shifter mages."

"Good the old Battle Crow even noticed," Kheladin growled and breathed a fiery gout of flames.

"She did more than notice. She cast a spell to disrupt our memories out of sheer meanness. If ye wouldna have reminded me… Hell, 'tis surprised I am we got here at all. The Celtic gods, Gwydion and Arawn, sent us to warn you and Lachlan. They told us their magic would trump the Morrigan's, but not forever." One corner of her mouth turned down. "'Twould appear I just ran up against *forever*. Or mayhap their magic got subverted by your wards."

"What impact has the Morrigan's mischief had on the rest of our kind?"

"Those in Fire Mountain are safe so long as they remain there. The memory-altering spell only snares them when they set foot on Earth."

"We just saw Gwydion, Arawn, and Ceridwen, and they dinna tell us aught of any such casting. Did they try to neutralize it?"

She cast a look Kheladin's way that said he should ask something worth her time answering.

Jonathan watched the exchange, chest tight with excitement, feeling he'd fallen into one of the old tales where heroes and heroines walked among humans.

"Let me try again." Kheladin sounded exasperated. "Did the Morrigan wake the black wyvern's mage, Rhukon?"

"'Twas the first thing she did."

"So all our effort was for naught." The dragon clanked his jaws together. "I must alert Lachlan. Where'd the Celts find you? And how long ago?"

Britta rolled her eyes. "Not in Fire Mountain, though I admit Tarika and I retreated there after Rhukon, Connor, and their dragons teamed with the Morrigan, and things werena looking good. Nay, the Celts plucked us out of the sixteen hundreds. They told us enough about what the future holds to alarm us and sent us on our way."

"Aye, and how long ago was that," Kheladin prodded."

"Mayhap a week. Tarika had things to attend to afore we could come. Why is that important?"

"Because Lachlan and I just sought them out, and they reminded us they doona censure their own, meaning they have no plans to clip the Battle Crow's wings."

"I believe I understand." Tarika forced her voice through Britta's vocal chords. "They rousted us out to excuse themselves from action. Craven bastards, the lot of them." Fire rolled from Britta's mouth.

"For the love of the goddess," she sputtered from around flames. "Stop that."

Kheladin inclined his head. "Though the circumstances leave much to be desired, thank you for coming."

A warm smile lit Britta's face. It softened her features and made her look barely more than a girl. Jonathan's cock stiffened where it pressed against his jeans. Breath caught in his throat, and he fought against touching her, running his hands down her golden skin. He drew magic around himself to mask his lust, make it unobtrusive, but she noticed anyway.

Britta turned an appraising glance his way. "Aye, ye'd do well to hide your rut from me."

Embarrassed at being caught out but curious too, he asked, "Why?"

She tossed her head at Kheladin. "Tell him, dragon. Mayhap he'll believe it if he hears it from another, ahem, *male*." Her last word dripped sarcasm.

Kheladin blew so much steam he looked like an old-fashioned train. Jonathan bristled. Worse, his cock wasn't in the mood for retreat. He tried for dignity. "Look. If it's all the same to you, I'd just as soon move on. I withdraw my question."

"Nay." Kheladin got his mirth under control. "Many have tried to mate with Tarika—and Britta too. I believe they fancy themselves reincarnations of Artemis—or Arianrhod or Hecate. 'Tis why they bonded one to the other."

Jonathan's brows crawled up his forehead. "Those three are all virgin huntresses."

"Good ye know your mythology." Kheladin clanged his jaws shut for a second time.

"I thought you were Celtic," Jonathan sputtered. "Artemis was Greek. Hecate too."

Kheladin bathed him in smoke until he bent over coughing. "Arianrhod is Celtic. I picked Artemis because ye might recognize her. Most of our goddesses have fallen out of human memory. How Britta is isna entirely her fault, though."

She put her hands on her hips and glared. Breasts peeked through a curtain of hair. "I'm not sure whether to thank you or let Tarika out to throttle you. How would I have had the time to either find a mate or attend to him once found?"

"Lachlan dinna have a wife, either." Kheladin's tone was mild.

"Aye, but he fucked enough women to make up for it." Britta narrowed her eyes. "As I recall, there was a string of housekeepers in addition to a bevy of local maids."

"He was laird of Clan Moncrieffe. 'Twas natural enough maids would wish to be his lady." Kheladin defended his shifter bondmate.

Jonathan felt as if he'd wandered in at the midpoint of a very old argument. He cleared his throat. "Was there a specific reason neither dragon shifter wed?"

Britta snorted. "Ye know nothing of what it takes to become a dragon shifter. I studied long—as did Lachlan—and forsook much. A man would've only gotten in my way, as would bairns. I could've made certain I dinna conceive, but what man doesna wish heirs?"

Kheladin leaned closer to Jonathan. "Her da was a powerful mage and laird of Cumbria. Many a swain wished to share her bed —and her dowry."

"Men! Cretins, the lot of them!" Britta threw a hand in the air, screwing her face into a disgusted moue. She spun and strode toward where Kheladin indicated Lachlan's clothing chest was.

Jonathan cleared his throat and sent a thought to Kheladin since he didn't want to be the butt of Britta's scorn. *"Temperamental, isn't she?"*

"Ye doona know the half of it, laddie. Yet she is courageous—and compassionate. 'Twasna accidental the gods picked her to assist us."

"Guess I'll wait until she's dressed and then take her into Inverness. We can find more clothes, some shoes, and a meal."

"Aye, and then ye must return. Doona tarry overlong. While ye're gone, I'll raise Lachlan."

"Whatever are the two of you whispering about in mind speech? Sounds like a buzzing beehive over there." Britta sashayed to them wrapped in a cream-colored linen shirt that fell just south of her groin. A pair of black tights draped over her arm.

Jonathan eyed her. "Are you going to put those on?"

She focused her golden eyes on him and slowly, deliberately, shook out the tights and rolled one leg. Still watching him intently, she raised her leg, giving him a clear view of tight red-gold curls, before she shoved it into the woolen pants. Heat raced through him, so intense he could barely breathe. His cock strained against his pants. For one long, awkward moment, he was afraid he'd come in his shorts.

For Christ's sake. I haven't had this much trouble controlling myself since I was a teenager twenty years ago.

Because he couldn't force himself to look away, he squeezed his eyes shut and thought about breathing. Just breathing. Not about burying himself to the hilt inside her glorious pussy. His cock jerked. It didn't want breathing. It wanted fucking and reminded him it had been months since he paid any attention to his sexual needs.

Time passed. Kheladin's energy pulsed to one side. Jonathan could pick out witches he knew from how their psychic emanations felt.

Maybe I should get one of the women to feed her and get her some shoes...

"Och aye, and that wouldna be nearly this much fun," she purred.

He ground his teeth together until his jaw ached. At least it took his mind off his cock. "Stay out of my head. A man's thoughts need to be, well, private."

She ignored his plea. "Do ye think I'm dressed enough to be decent?" Her scent eddied closer, lavender, musk, and something he couldn't identify. Maybe amber. "Ye'll need to open those lovely eyes to answer me."

Her magic zinged into him, bypassing his wards as if they weren't there. He snapped his eyes wide open and took a couple steps back. "The only way this is going to work," he gritted out, "is if you stop teasing me with your body. It really is incredible, but I'm sure you already know that."

"Is it now? I've lived among dragons and our mages for so long, I'd nearly forgotten. But now ye are near and fawning, I find I've missed human attention."

"We all have," Kheladin cut in. "Yon lad has a point. His cock is ready to burst from his pants. If ye expect him to sit with you, share a meal and mayhap information about this era—about which ye know nothing, I might add—ye will need to behave more appropriately."

"I doona understand." Britta drew her perfect brows together. "He can tap a serving wench. Once his lust is satiated, he can return to my side."

Jonathan chuckled. "Ha! I always wondered what it was truly like a few hundred years back. There aren't too many handy *serving wenches* willing to lift their skirts—or drop their pants, more likely —these days. I'd have to wine them, dine them, at least pretend to care—"

She waved him to silence. "I'm starting to understand. I willna flaunt myself, though 'tis great fun to know I can still heat a man's blood."

Heat a man's blood, is it?

He bit back a laugh at the idea and the Gaelic inflection in his thoughts. For a moment, he'd sounded just like his da. "You do way more than that." He let himself look at her. The tights were in place, waist string tied, but she had yet to button the shirt. Apparently sensing his thoughts, she hastily looped square, wooden buttons into their holes.

She held her arms to the side and twirled in place. "There. Will I do?"

He found he could breathe again. Although still aroused, the desperate edge had receded. Jonathan nodded. "Yes. Your magic or mine?"

"Yours. I'm still depleted from my travels."

He glanced at Kheladin, now surrounded by ten witches, all patting and fussing over him. The dragon glowed beneath their attention, bathing the cave with his inner radiance.

"How soon do you need us back?" Jonathan asked, smothering a smile.

Kheladin suffused him in steam. "We covered that. I would verra much like to tell you to take your time, but I fear 'tis something we may well be running short of. Enjoy a meal. Find the lass some footwear and a warm jacket. Mayhap other clothes that fit her better. Then return."

"Ye can link to me if something untoward happens." Tarika borrowed Britta's vocal chords again, her voice deeper, metallic, resonant.

Kheladin included her in the steam bath. "'Tis been long since I've had another dragon—at least one on our side—near to hand. Thanks to you again for coming."

"My pleasure." Britta's voice was her own again. "Once we return, Tarika says we must alter our bond so we may enjoy the freedom of our respective bodies, like ye and Lachlan." She turned to Jonathan. "I stand ready."

"Wait." Kheladin held up a foreleg and chanted a few notes mingled with fire. "There, my wards are open."

Jonathan threw his rucksack over a shoulder. He summoned magic. Once they were wrapped in his casting, he aimed for a thick grove in one of Inverness's many parks. If they got very lucky, they wouldn't disturb a couple in the midst of enjoying one another. The cave's walls glimmered, then thinned and turned to black as he ferried them away from Kheladin and the phalanx of adoring witches.

Providence was on his side. It was dim where he brought them out in a thick hawthorn grove. And cold. He slid his iPhone from a pocket and glanced at the time. Just closing on seven. Not so bad, except it meant they'd need to shop first, else the stores would shut for the night.

Britta inhaled noisily. "It smells odd." She drew closer to him. "Is the air poisoned?"

"It's just car exhaust. The air's better here than in a truly big city."

"*Car exhaust?* Neither word means aught."

Where to begin?

"Let's get you some clothes. I'll explain what I can over dinner. In the meantime, it might be best if you didn't ask too many questions."

She drew herself up and squared her shoulders. "And why not?"

"You don't want people to think you're odd. Or that you don't belong here."

A shiver ran through her body. He glanced down and saw her shift from one bare foot to the next on chill, damp ground. "Come on." He hooked a hand beneath her arm and tugged. "Shoes first. Then clothes."

She fell into step beside him. "They'll have to measure me. It takes several days to craft a pair of boots."

"Not anymore. We'll find what you need readymade."

"Really? Will the quality be acceptable?"

Spoken like a true Countess.

"Probably not, but you'll make do. It's better than being cold and barefoot." He tightened his hold on her arm, wanting to protect her, care for her. It would take her time to get used to the modern world —if she stayed here long enough to learn about it. Jonathan examined the feelings coursing through him. Was it possible she'd snared him in some sort of spell?

"I did no such thing." Enough outrage ran beneath her words, he believed her.

"Look here." He kept his voice low. "You have to stay out of my thoughts."

"But how else will I know about them? About you?"

He chuckled. "How about if you ask me questions and satisfy yourself with what I'm willing to share. Turn this way." He pushed open a swinging door and followed her into a brightly lit shoe store. He blinked a few times to ease the transition from daylight to fluorescent lighting.

She shielded her eyes with a hand. "What manner of magic creates light this strong?"

"Hush. We call it electricity. Come on." He guided her to a display rack and selected a serviceable pair of lace up boots. "What do you think of these?"

She wrinkled her nose. "They're ugly and shoddily made." She flicked a loose thread with a fingertip.

"Then you pick something."

She glanced about and trailed her hands over tennis shoes and sandals as she walked through the store. After *oohing* and *aahing* over several pairs of high heels, she let him guide her back to the place they'd begun.

"Britta. It's summer, but the nights are always on the chilly side. Your feet will get cold unless you get sturdy boots and socks. How about if we try these." He pointed. "And those." He pointed again.

"I suppose ye're right. Do ye think either could be dyed black?"

A clerk had been hovering. "We have that style in black, ma'am. What size should I get for you?" He glanced down and inhaled audibly. "B-but you're barefoot. Your feet must be freezing."

Color stained Britta's cheeks. "'Tisn't so bad as all that, laddie. Not when ye have dragon's—"

"My sister's joking," Jonathan cut in fast. "She's always had quite the sense of humor."

Britta shot him a look that could kill, but at least she didn't say anything else.

He closed his hand around her arm and gave it a warning squeeze, hoping she'd understand not to contradict his next words. "My sister just gave birth. Err, twins. Her feet got bigger. Much bigger. Nothing fits but her house slippers, and she was too embarrassed to wear them. How about if you measure her?"

"Certainly. If you'd just sit over there?" The clerk gestured to a bank of chairs.

Britta followed the clerk, but not before spearing Jonathan with another aggravated look.

An hour later, they had two pairs of shoes—one black, one brown—socks, underwear, three pairs of warm corduroy pants, sweaters, T-shirts, and two jackets. Jonathan was a thousand pounds poorer but considered the funds well spent. She stopped trying to seduce him from the moment they left Kheladin's cave, which meant he could simply enjoy her company.

She led the way out of the clothing store he'd selected after they finished with the shoe store and turned to him. "Can we get something to eat now?" Both of them were laden with bags.

"Sure. What do you feel like?"

She leaned close. "I doona know. Everything here is so strange, I feel I'm playacting, yet without knowing my lines. Pick something. Simple food and stiff spirits."

"Have you heard anything from Kheladin?"

She shook her head. "Nay, but Tarika isna pleased. She believes we waste valuable time. 'Tis possible she'll settle once we find food. She's hungry."

Jonathan considered their options. He didn't want to bring her to a noisy pub where they'd have to strain to hear one another. Nor did he want a nightclub. He looked up and down one of Inverness' main streets until his gaze settled on a smallish place where a sign promised *Excellent Food In An Intimate Atmosphere.*

It sounded perfect.

"Let's try over there. Maybe we'll have enough privacy for me to answer some of those questions I've seen dancing behind your eyes."

She smiled at him. Really smiled without coquettish edges. "Ye've been truly kind to me. I apologize for…well, for how I was earlier. I shouldna have been such a tease."

"Apology accepted. I do understand, though."

She cocked her head to one side. "Do ye?"

He grinned. "Sure. Sex is power. Or it can be. But being friends is better."

She grinned back. "To friendship, then. Find us a bottle, and we can drink to it."

CHAPTER 3

A black-suited servant greeted them at the door of the eating establishment, and Britta followed him toward the back of the room. It was quite dark, and she raised a hand to summon her mage light. Jonathan, apparently intuiting what she was about, dropped a warning hand onto her shoulder.

"Don't." He spoke the word into her mind.

She dropped her hand to her side. *"How can all these people live in a world without magic?"*

"Good question," Tarika hissed. The dragon rolled restlessly deep within her. *"The Celts sent us to do something important. Our survival hangs in the balance, and ye waste time shopping. Pfft. We must confer with Lachlan and Kheladin. I wish to know more of their new bond and—"*

"Ssht. We will speak of this once we've eaten."

"Ye canna dismiss me. I am one of the First Born. I will force my way out." Tarika writhed in Britta's chest and belly, pushing hard against their bond.

"Look about us. Ye wouldna fit. The door is too small. We would have to break out a wall to leave this place. Plus, we havena eaten yet." Britta held her breath. Tarika could be cantankerous, but this time she

withdrew, muttering imprecations. Thank the goddess the dragon hadn't forced smoke—or worse, fire—through Britta's throat.

The servant drew a chair back for her, and she dropped into it. "If ye could find somewhere for all these?" She pointed to the bags piled atop her lap.

The man shrugged apologetically. "I'm not certain they'd be safe beneath the coatrack. But if madam wishes…"

"It's all right. We'll just stack them in the corner." Jonathan emptied his arms and then scooped the bags out of her lap and added them to the pile. He balanced his rucksack atop everything before sitting down.

The servant handed them stiff placards with undecipherable writing. She opened her mouth to ask something, but Jonathan nudged her leg under the table. "We'll need a moment," he told the servant.

"Aye." She waved a dismissive hand. "Doona return until we summon you."

"Really?" The servant seemed to remember his place after his comment. He bowed slightly and said, "As madam wishes," before turning to walk away.

Britta bent closer. "Cheeky fellow for a servant."

Jonathan moved his chair so he sat close enough to whisper into her ear. "He's not a servant. He's a waiter and he works here—for wages and tips."

"Nevertheless, he's of the inferior classes."

"Um, we don't think that way anymore."

She propped her head on an upraised hand. "Och aye, I need a drink."

"They have a full bar here. What would you like?"

"Irish whiskey."

Jonathan caught the waiter's eye. The man trotted over. "Sir?"

"Irish whiskey for the lady, best one on your shelf. I'd like a single malt scotch, at least twenty years old…"

Britta tried to follow their conversation but felt lost after the first few words. The men bandied unfamiliar names about, as they argued the merits of various aging methods. Apparently, the family distilleries she was familiar with had long since quit producing spirits. Though she'd done a good job masking her shock, she was appalled at what passed for life in whatever year she was in. The air smelled bad. She'd taken a sip of water from some sort of flexible bottle Jonathan had in his rucksack while they were in one of the shops, and it held the same toxic undertones as the air.

The waiter withdrew. Jonathan scanned the placard with writing on it. "What do you think you want?"

She bit her lip, feeling defensive and ashamed. "'Tis not that I canna read," she whispered, "yet these words make no sense to me."

He laid a hand over hers. "I can see where they wouldn't. Language has changed a lot. Would you prefer fish, beef, chicken, or maybe just rice or noodles in a sauce?"

"Beef. Bread. Greens."

Jonathan nodded. "Would those greens be cooked or raw?"

"Doesna matter."

The waiter returned with two shot glasses. Britta frowned. "My, but 'tis only a wee bit in the glass. Mayhap, ye should bring the bottle and have done with it."

The waiter's eyes widened. "Madam. It's five pounds, six for a shot of the aged whiskey your husband ordered."

"He isna my—"

"You heard the lady," Jonathan broke in. "Bring the bottle. While you're at it, we'd like two tenderloin steaks, rare, with the mixed green salad and bread."

"Very good, sir." The man bowed slightly and was gone.

"Ye dinna have to order more spirits. They're verra dear." Britta picked her glass up and raised it. "To friendship." She tipped the shot glass back and drank half.

"To friendship, indeed." Jonathan took a sip of his scotch.

"Ye barely drank anything," she noted.

He nodded. "You're observant. I have to stay alert. This environment is unfamiliar to you."

She set her glass down. "Thanks, but I scarcely need a caretaker. Five pounds is a vast amount. Why, ye could buy a good-sized herd of cows for far less."

He smiled. "Not anymore. I believe there are about fourteen shots in a fifth of whiskey."

She added up pence and shillings, appalled. "Seventy pounds for the bottle and 'tisn't counting the six pence times fourteen additional. Ach. I'm wondering how much my new clothes cost."

"It doesn't matter. I have enough money and very little to spend it on. Your math skills are quite sharp." He took another sip of scotch. She drained her glass, enjoying the feel of the liquor burning its way down her throat to her stomach. The whiskey wasn't bad, but it suffered from the same thing everything else did: an odd under taste. Try as she might, she couldn't determine what the underlying grain was.

The waiter thumped a fresh bottle in front of Jonathan. At his nod, he stripped off the seal with a small knife and left, returning moments later with two plates heaped with raw greens and what looked like shaved cheese.

"Pepper, madam?" The waiter brandished a wooden container.

"Nay."

"Sir?" Jonathan nodded and the waiter twisted the wooden decanter. The sharp smell of ground spice tickled Britta's nose.

Once the waiter left, she picked up her fork and began eating. The greens were fresh enough but tasted bland. Not like what she remembered at all. "Whatever is wrong with the food?" she demanded.

Jonathan shrugged. "Chemicals they use to grow it. Overused soil. Water contaminated with agricultural products."

"Ye may as well be speaking Greek. How can ye stand to live here?"

"It's all I've ever known."

"Aye, makes sense." She returned her attention to the greens. They ate in silence until their plates were empty. She poured more whiskey and waggled the bottle at him.

He shook his head. "No. Like I said earlier, one of us needs a clear head. I have to make certain nothing gets in the way of us returning to Kheladin."

Her gaze softened. "Ye're taking care of me. I sniped at you about it a little bit ago, but I canna remember when anyone beyond Tarika has done aught for me since I was a girl."

Jonathan sucked in a breath. "Maybe you never let them."

She smiled crookedly and tilted her chin up. "Touché. Mayhap we could speak of other things."

He looked right through her with his glowing witch's eyes, although the more time she spent with him, the less like a witch he felt.

"Getting a bit too close to home, eh?" He quirked a brow. "Looks as if you're off the hook. Our dinner's here."

She craned her neck and glanced over one shoulder. Sure enough, the waiter, laden with a large tray, headed toward them. Her stomach growled at the rich, meaty aroma, but she welcomed the diversion. The conversation had taken a decidedly personal turn, and it made her uncomfortable. The witch—or whatever he was—read her far too easily for comfort. She'd have to do a better job shielding her thoughts.

She'd eaten about half her steak when Jonathan asked, "What was going on when we walked back to our table?"

For a moment, her mind was blank. "I doona quite know what ye mean."

He bent close and spoke low into her ear. "When we were following the waiter to this table, you were talking to someone. I couldn't make out the words, yet I felt the telepathy magic."

"Och aye." She turned her head, positioning her lips close to his ear. "'Tis the Morrigan's memory curse, to be sure. Tarika wasna pleased. 'Twas she I conversed with."

"Does she sense something amiss?"

"Nay. She was worried we wasted time and wanted to return to Kheladin and Lachlan with all due haste."

Desire for knowledge flickered in his eyes. "How'd you talk her out of it?"

"I dinna. We merely put it off until after we'd eaten. She's as hungry as I am. If it was up to her, we'd take to the skies, locate likely prey, and feast on a cow or sheep."

"Good thing you didn't. The farmers around here take their herds and flocks seriously. It would be a good way to get yourselves shot."

"Ye canna shoot an arrow so high as we fly."

He laid a hand over hers. "I wasn't talking about arrows. I was talking about bullets. And high-powered hunting rifles. They've improved substantially since the muskets you probably remember." He hesitated a beat. "What year did you and Tarika leave Earth for Fire Mountain?"

She returned to her steak, thinking. "The middle of the eighteenth century. I canna remember the precise year. 'Tis a miracle I even recall that much. We tired of Fire Mountain after a while, though, and returned to the sixteen hundreds."

"Why then?"

She shrugged. "'Twas one of my favorite times. Tarika's too. There was enough modernity to take the edge off the ignorance of the Dark Ages, yet people still believed in magic—and dragons."

"This reminds me of my conversation with Kheladin." Jonathan looked thoughtful. "There's a fine balance point between science and those like us, er you."

"Ye had it right the first time. 'Twould be *us*."

He resumed eating and finished his scotch, pouring a dribble from the whiskey bottle into his empty glass. "Just wanted to taste it." He smiled.

Britta looked at him, really looked at him, and liked what she saw. Classic facial bone structure, with a high forehead, sculpted cheekbones, and strong, square jaw, hosted expressive eyes and full lips. Very straight, white teeth were visible when he smiled. Dark stubble dotted his cheeks, and his hair was braided in one of the ancient Celtic warrior patterns. Whatever manner of mage he was, she hadn't seen the like of him in a very long time. She swept her gaze downward, taking in broad shoulders, slender hips, and long legs, which disappeared beneath the table. She squirmed a bit as unfamiliar sensations coursed through her.

He got an odd look on his face and moved his chair a few inches away. "You promised not to do that."

"Aye. Sorry." She felt her face heat and reached for the basket of bread and a small tub of butter.

I'm aroused. I want him.

Breath caught in her throat. She'd never felt anything beyond mild curiosity about what a man's body might be like, but she wanted to remove Jonathan's jacket, unbutton his shirt, and run her fingers over the skin beneath.

Jonathan watched her with a sidelong gaze. Something between them had shifted a few moments before. He'd felt her scrutiny and then a stab of heat as his cock came alive with lust. It wasn't like in Kheladin's cave, though. She was aroused too. He sensed it, smelled it, saw the way she averted her eyes. If she truly was a virgin, she'd have found ways to sidestep her sexuality, bottle it up. Yet she was blushing like a schoolgirl and very interested in buttering a slice of bread—twice.

"I think you can probably eat it." He grinned. "If you put any more butter on it, it'll crumble to shreds."

"Ye dinna have to say aught. If ye were well-bred, ye would've remained silent." She stuffed half the bread into her mouth and chewed furiously.

He tried to swallow laughter and failed. When he could talk

again, he sidled his chair even closer to hers. "What? If I were a gentleman, or some such archaic description of how men are supposed to behave, I wouldn't have noticed your, um, interest in me?"

She nodded. Her face got redder still. "We should finish our meal."

"I've had nearly all I want." He waged a brief battle with common sense and lost. "I'm much more interested in how you're feeling about me. You spent a while just looking me over. Did you like what you saw?"

"Och!" She cut more meat, then chewed it and swallowed quickly. "Men! The lot of you are impossible. All you think about is what's between your legs."

The waiter had been headed their way. Jonathan saw him spin and walk quickly in the opposite direction. Poor man. First Britta treated him like trash, and now he'd overheard something that didn't comprise most people's notion of polite supper conversation. Not good. The idea was for them to blend in, not become the waiter's prime conversational gambit once he went off shift.

Jonathan reached for the whiskey bottle and ran his hands over places he'd seen the waiter touch. He gathered enough of the man's essence to send a spell his way.

"Whatever are ye up to?" Britta sopped up the last of the meat juice on her plate with the last piece of bread.

"The waiter overheard too much of our conversation. I simply made certain he'd forget about us."

She grinned. "Would it include him forgetting to collect for our food and drink?"

"Now there's a fine idea. It wasn't in my mind at the time, but—" Jonathan held up a hand in response to the shocked expression on her face. "Never fear. I'm planning to leave money on the table for what we ate. I've never stiffed an establishment yet, and I'm not starting now."

She blew out a breath. "Thanks be to Ceridwen. 'Tis bad luck to cheat."

He patted her hand. "Good. I have someone to keep me on the straight and narrow. Are you finished?" She nodded, and he dug for his wallet, counting out pound notes and adding a generous tip. The waiter wouldn't remember them, but he would know this had been his table. "What do you want to do with the rest of the whiskey?"

"I've had enough. I suppose we could bring it along with the other things we bought."

He located the stopper and placed it back atop the bottle, hoping it wouldn't spill. Britta was already on her feet, gathering shopping bags into her arms. He picked up his rucksack and the rest of the shopping bags, before following her out into the evening. The street was much quieter than it had been when they entered the restaurant. Light was finally fading from the long summer day. It had to be around ten-thirty, maybe even eleven. People still strolled up and down the boulevard, some alone, more arm-in-arm with someone they cared about.

"Can we travel from here?" she asked.

He'd been so taken by her beauty, he hadn't noticed her voice before. It was rich and low with musical under notes. Jonathan felt her spell take shape. People were passing them, so he answered her telepathically. *"No. We can't just disappear. Come on. We'll go back to the park where we started."* He wanted to take her arm, but his hands were full.

She looked about. "Which way? I canna remember."

Illuminated by a nearby streetlight, her face was so beautiful and so vulnerable, it touched his heart—and drew him like a magnet. He stopped thinking. Bending his head, he closed his mouth over hers and waited for the fireworks.

She didn't slap him, though. Didn't even draw away. Instead, she opened her mouth to his kiss and, unbelievably, kissed him back. She tasted sweet like the Irish whiskey, and her tongue tangled with his when he deepened their kiss. Jonathan wanted to drop the shopping bags crushed between them so he could wrap his arms around her and feel her body pressed against his.

His breathing quickened. So did hers.

"Well, well. Terribly convenient you're here, dragon," a deep, accented male voice purred from behind them. "And a bonus to boot."

Jonathan jumped away from Britta. He raised his hands to draw power, and the bags in his arms crashed to the pavement. He heard the whiskey bottle shatter, and the pungent scent of spirits sharpened the damp air. He spun and narrowed his eyes, raking the area around him to see who'd spoken, but he couldn't locate a man who matched the voice. He felt wickedness, though. The air was heavy with putrid smells, dead things left to rot.

Passersby scattered like rats, gagging as they fled.

Magic thrummed, hot and intense. Jonathan's mouth went dry. He cursed his total lack of experience. He'd never faced a magical enemy, never expected to. Worse, he'd ignored classes the coven offered in self-defense, figuring they'd be a waste of time.

Looks as if I'm about to pay for my arrogance—and my lack of foresight.

He was focusing his magic, getting ready to release it toward where evil felt thickest, when a ripping, tearing noise grated. He snapped his head around, hunting for its source.

What the hell was that?

Britta's clothes lay in shreds. Tarika blazed into being. The dragon lifted him with her forelegs and plunked him onto her back. "Hang on, witch, or whatever ye are. I canna battle Rhukon and watch out for you." Her leathery red wings pumped the air, and the city's streets fell away.

Jesus Christ on a fucking crutch, I'm flying. On a dragon.

Wonder trumped fear. Jonathan made a grab for horns, which grew at the base of Tarika's neck, and held on for dear life.

The biggest crow Jonathan had ever seen rose out of nowhere, blotting out half the sky. The Morrigan. Raucous cawing blasted him. Pain lanced through his skull as his eardrums ruptured, and fluid sluiced down his cheeks.

When the Battle Crow spoke, it sounded as if she were underwater. "Ye'll face me, dragon shifter. Rhukon insisted on accosting you, but his blundering has begun to annoy me." The Morrigan focused her beady, avian gaze on Jonathan. "'Tis only the beginning, puny human. Afore I'm done, ye'll wish ye were dead."

Fury roiled through him. Jonathan had never wanted to kill anything before, but he wanted the thing hovering before them dead. More than dead. Annihilated.

"Hang onto that thought." Tarika's mind voice sounded grim. *"We're going to try to lose her."*

CHAPTER 4

*P*ower buffeted him from all sides. It sizzled in the air and stung his eyes and nose. The dragon dove and banked, avoiding bolts of magic from the Morrigan and spraying the Battle Crow with flames. The smell of singed feathers was thick, but the bird didn't catch fire, no doubt employing magic to keep herself safe. He pulled a ward around himself, realized he couldn't project magic through it, and let it fall. There had to be a better use for his untrained abilities. He sounded a telepathic alarm. The witches in Kheladin's cave might not be able to hear through the dragon's warding, but any witch within a ten-kilometer radius would respond and come to their aid.

He peered down. Surely the constabulary would respond to the ruckus, but Jonathan couldn't see Inverness at all. It was as if they'd moved to a different plane. He couldn't hear the city, either. Maybe the clash and crash of battle drowned everything else out, but he suspected Scotland was a long way from wherever the Morrigan and Tarika were duking it out.

"Doona just sit there like a great dolt. Help me."

The dragon's voice startled him. "Tarika?"

"Who the fuck else? The Morrigan sure as hell willna bother talking with you."

She already had, but Jonathan didn't waste words pointing it out. He started to protest he didn't know the first thing about warfare but shut his mouth. He wanted Britta—and her dragon—to respect him, not see him as worthless baggage. Jonathan reached for his magic, relieved it was more-or-less intact. "Tell me what to do."

"Open your mind. Add your power to mine."

It took a bit of maneuvering, but Jonathan experimented with frequencies until he felt the dragon slam into him. The linkage was a two-way street. Memories from thousands of years boiled furiously in Tarika's head, right alongside her hatred for the Morrigan. Her current strategy was as clear as if she'd told him with words. Tarika wanted to open a time portal, sequester them inside, and bar the Morrigan. From there they could escape to anywhere.

Sounds at least possible. "We need to divert her."

Dragon laughter nearly deafened his already-battered hearing. "How?"

A particularly rocky aerial maneuver unseated him, and he bounced half a meter off her back. "*Ooph.*" Jonathan landed hard and gripped Tarika tighter, determined not to create more problems for them. His next thought nearly flattened him. It was so obvious, he felt like an idiot for not realizing it sooner.

By the goddess! This is just like the games I design.

But they're not real.

So? They depend on strategy. Besides, it's not as if there are dozens of choices here.

He turned his attention to Tarika. "*Can the Morrigan hear us if we use telepathic speech?*"

"*If she weren't expending so much effort fighting us, yes. As things stand, I doona believe so.*"

Tarika coiled magic more tightly around them and burrowed even deeper into his head. Jonathan tensed his muscles, extending as much power as he had to give. Time slid past as dragon and crow traded blows that would've been lethal were the two combatants not immortal.

This isn't going to work. We'll never gain the upper hand long enough to escape.

He expected the dragon to argue, so he couched his words as a statement, not open for discussion. *"I'm going to sever my link with you. Once that's done, I'll draw magic and transport myself back to Inverness. If my strategy works, the Morrigan will see me as easy pickings and follow me, figuring she can always track you down later."*

Tarika spewed fire at the Morrigan and banked hard right. *"Hmm...Might work if we—"*

"I doona want you to sacrifice yourself." Britta's voice rose over Tarika's.

"Be reasonable," Jonathan retorted, touched she cared what happened to him, yet knowing now wasn't the time for *that* discussion. *"So long as we remain together, we'll just keep trading pot shots with the Morrigan until one of us falls out of the sky, exhausted. Even if that abomination of a Celtic goddess doesn't follow me, I can find my way back to Kheladin's and raise the alarm."*

Power jolted Tarika. She screamed her outrage—and her pain. Jonathan didn't wait for further dialogue. He slammed his mind shut. Drenching himself in power, he imagined the hawthorn grove in the park. The sensation of falling created vertigo, and his head spun crazily. He'd never engaged traveling magic while airborne.

Holy shit! What if it doesn't work?

It has to.

As a laggardly second thought, he diverted some of the magic surrounding him into as impenetrable a ward as he could create. The darkness around him grayed at the edges. Soon, he'd either come out where he planned or come face-to-face with an ugly surprise he could only guess at.

"No more desultory playing at witchcraft," he muttered. "If the goddess gets me out of this one, I swear I'll read every fucking grimoire I can get my hands on."

He felt the ground's approach as a magnetic pulling sensation before he actually saw it. Jonathan drew his knees up and tucked his arms around them, just in time to roll into a landing. He connected hard with the earth but nothing broke. The second he could, he sprang to his feet, hands raised to summon power in case the Battle Crow was hot on his heels.

"Jonathan!" a man cried.

"Christ, mate. We heard your alarm. Where the fuck were you?" a woman shouted.

"Aye, and are ye expecting company?" another woman asked in a strong Scottish brogue.

Half a dozen witches closed around him. Relief surged. They'd heard his frantic call from wherever he and Tarika had been. "How'd you find me?"

Caty, a broad-shouldered witch with black hair that came to her knees, stepped forward. Head of one of the local covens, she wore power like she owned it. Her green eyes snapped. "What danger do you face, witch? To call us out on false pretenses..." Her voice faded, and she angled her gaze toward a ragged hole forming in the night air.

"Crap!" the man cursed.

"Battle lines," Caty commanded.

Jonathan watched in amazement as the witches formed a half circle and dragged him into their formation right next to Caty. This coven had apparently practiced. Before tomorrow came, he'd make certain his coven at least had a plan in place—assuming he was still alive.

"What manner of being is that?" Caty jabbed him with an elbow and pointed upward.

"The Morrigan."

She rolled her eyes. "Oh please. I'll see you're stripped of every— Holy fucking godhead."

The Battle Crow broke through and hovered in the air before

Jonathan, cawing raucously. "Found you. Not that it was even minimally difficult."

He slammed himself sideways in the nick of time. The Morrigan would've annihilated him from twenty feet away if he hadn't moved out of her path. As it was, he gulped air and rocked back on the balls of his feet, reeling from the strength of her blow.

He skinned his lips back from his teeth in a feral grin. His strategy had worked! Tarika and Britta must be well on their way to safety.

"I see ye found reinforcements," the Morrigan taunted. "They look too little and too late to me."

Jonathan squared his shoulders. "Only because you're not looking at the big picture. There are more where these came from. Be gone, Celt. You're an embarrassment to your fellow gods."

"What did ye say?" Wingbeats brought her almost beak to nose with him.

Caty and her witches wove power around Jonathan. The added support warmed his heart and fueled his courage.

"I said be gone. Kheladin told us your fellow gods are disgusted with your antics and appalled by your alliance with the black and red wyverns." He glanced at the witches ranged round him. "We are seven. It's a power number. You cannot hope to prevail."

In support of his words, Caty chanted, summoning destruction. The rest of the witches joined in at proscribed intervals. Jonathan recognized the incantation. It opened a gateway to the nether regions. At the spell's end, a demon would appear and ask to do their bidding. Apparently, the Morrigan recognized the casting too.

"Ye havena seen the last of me." The Crow snapped her beak, slashed him with it, and was gone.

Searing pain ripped through his face. The smell of blood, hot and coppery, filled his nostrils.

Christ! What'd she do to me?

He raised a hand to his face, shocked his warding hadn't even slowed her down, and fingered a gash from his cheekbone to his jawline.

"Och, doona be touchin' it," the witch with the strong Scottish burr screeched.

"We can heal you," Caty muttered. "Stand still. While we're patching you up, tell us how it is you came to piss off the Morrigan."

"If you're going to heal me," Jonathan sagged against her, "start with my ears so I can at least hear you. Both drums are ruptured."

"Ye sent him to his death," Britta screeched. Fury pounded through her, but she was helpless inside the dragon.

"We doona know. Not for certain. Let us leave while we can. We canna help him—or anyone else from here."

"Return us to Kheladin's cave."

"I planned to retreat to Fire Mountain."

"Nay. Not until we're certain of Jonathan's fate. He offered himself in our place. So long as he lives, we must do all we can to help him. We canna do aught from Fire Mountain. Besides, we made a promise to the Celtic gods."

The dragon grumbled, but Britta knew she'd capitulate. Tarika had a strong sense of honor, and Britta reminded her of a vow they made. *"The witch was brave,"* she added slyly.

Tarika blew fire and pulled magic to return them to the outskirts of Kheladin's wards. *"Aye. He surprised me. I wasna in favor of bringing him with us when I realized we were under attack."*

"Thank you for indulging me."

The dragon paused a beat. *"He is...attractive."*

"Aye. Beyond his physical charms, he has a good heart and a beautiful soul. Power to burn as well. I doona quite understand what I'm feeling—or exactly what he is—but I wish to explore it further."

They hurtled toward Inverness with Tarika chuckling and blowing smoke. *"Are ye thinking we've been maids long enough?"*

If Britta had been in her body, she would've blushed. The thought of admitting a man to her secret places was intriguing—and scary. So long as it was just her and Tarika, there were no worries about ceding power to another. Goddess knew, she and the dragon had enough arguments about who ran the show. Men—at least the variety she'd known in earlier times—expected to rule everything under their purview. Wives included.

Humph. Mayhap this isna a good idea. I doona need a master, no matter how drawn I am to him.

"Who wishes entrance past my wards?" Kheladin's mind voice boomed.

"We are returned," Tarika announced in response to the other dragon's query. "Let us in but be certain to drop the wards only long enough to admit us."

They melted through earth, and the walls of Kheladin's cave formed around them. Witches milled about in small groups, vying for choice spots near Kheladin. A striking man with thick, tawny hair and eyes the same green as Kheladin's stood next to the dragon with his arm around a woman who looked like a Viking princess.

Lachlan and his mate.

Tarika made her way to Kheladin's side and inclined her head. "Lachlan." She bathed him and his woman—and a few nearby witches—in steam. Britta cringed, hoping the blonde-haired woman wouldn't mind.

"Tarika." Lachlan narrowed his eyes. "Tell us what happened."

"Aye," Kheladin cut in. "Where's the witch, or whatever he is, who went with you?"

"Let me out," Britta demanded. "Ye can huddle with Kheladin telepathically and learn what transpired since we left. Ye can also get the exact wording for the casting that will allow us the freedom of our own bodies."

"Aye." Tarika ceded their form to Britta. "'Twould be much more convenient."

Britta reclaimed her body and shook herself. *Damn! Still naked.* All the shopping had been nothing but a colossal waste of time.

"Here." The Viking shucked a rucksack. She pulled a jacket out of it and handed it to Britta. "I'm Maggie Hibbins." She extended a hand, her sea-blue eyes twinkling merrily. "We'll have to find you some clothes. Shouldn't be a problem since we're close to the same size."

Britta stared at the extended hand. What was she supposed to do? Kiss it? She wasn't a man.

Lachlan grinned. "'Tis a modern custom. Ye take her hand, squeeze, but not too hard, and give it a shake."

"Aye." She grasped Maggie's hand. "I am Britta Kilkerran. My dragon is Tarika, though she would probably say I am her human. Och, but ye're warm."

"Not as warm as you, dragon shifter. Funny, Lachlan said the same thing about Kheladin. Let me rustle through Lachlan's chest. Maybe I can come up with something for your bottom half."

Britta held up a hand. "'Tisn't important. We must help Jonathan."

Lachlan quirked a brow. "The witch Kheladin asked after?" At Britta's nod, a knowing look stole over his face. "And why would the Iron Maid have even a sliver of interest in any man?"

"Iron Maid?" Maggie looked confused.

Britta snorted. "Och aye, and was that what ye called me behind my back all these years?"

Lachlan had the grace to look sheepish. "Sorry, lass. It just slipped out."

"Like the garments, 'tisn't important. I had clothes. Jonathan bought them for me, and a meal too. We were just returning when Rhukon appeared out of nowhere, followed by the Morrigan."

Maggie closed her teeth over her lower lip and drew closer to Lachlan, who snarled his annoyance.

"That sorry piece of dung," he said and spat onto the dirt floor of the cave. "I knew we hadna seen the end of her—or Rhukon. But I dinna expect them quite so soon. I left Rhukon asleep back in the fifteen hundreds—and not all that long ago."

"The Morrigan woke him." Kheladin was apparently following their conversation as well as his internal one with Tarika. "I was getting ready to tell you when Tarika rattled my wards."

"So, ye'd just arrived here?" Britta asked.

"Aye. Not five minutes afore you," Lachlan concurred.

"We were having supper when Kheladin said we had to come," Maggie added.

"Ye missed supper. I ruined one set of clothes and left several more stewing in a broken bottle of decent whiskey." Britta shrugged. "No matter. We're together to fight another day. 'Tis far more important than creature comforts."

"We must break our bond." Tarika spoke into her mind.

"What?" Anxiety gripped her, narrowing her throat.

"To be like Lachlan and Kheladin. They used a different magic, and a much more powerful one. We canna do the same until we are free of our current binding."

Britta started breathing again. Not being linked to Tarika was unthinkable. The dragon was so much a part of her, sometimes she forgot the days when she'd been a maid, and dragonless.

"Forgive me. I was eavesdropping." Lachlan half-bowed.

"At least have the decency to look ashamed." Maggie rolled her eyes.

"As I was saying," Lachlan broke in smoothly. "A bit of history is in order. Rhukon shanghaied us back to a hundred years afore Kheladin and I had bonded. Once we separated, the bond broke—"

"Because it hadna yet happened," Britta murmured.

"Aye. In the meantime, Kheladin did a bit of digging and came up with a much older version of the binding."

"The original one." Kheladin sounded smug.

"Tarika and I can alter how we're joined once we've done what we can to help Jonathan," Britta said. "His courage is what freed us.

The Morrigan took the bait he offered and went after him, allowing Tarika to escape."

"Och aye." Lachlan drew his brows together. "It doesna bode well."

Britta's heart felt like a lead weight in her chest. She'd known, but hearing it spoken aloud was like a death knell.

Maggie took her hand. "Maybe it's not as hopeless as you fear." Her voice and touch were comforting, almost hypnotic.

"Doona be using your magic on me, witch." Britta tried to pull her hand back, but Maggie held fast.

"I haven't used a shred. I'm a doctor, a psychiatrist. I've spent hours upon hours soothing troubled souls."

Truth pinged, bright and clean, off her magic. Britta sucked in a breath. *One less thing to worry about.* The last thing she needed was to alienate Lachlan's mate. "Sorry. I dinna mean to be so sharp."

"I understand completely." Maggie caught her gaze. "Truly I do."

"Someone comes." Kheladin sounded grim.

"Aye," Lachlan concurred. "I feel a disturbance in your wards."

Britta sent her own magic hurtling upward. She wasn't linked to Kheladin's warding, but if Rhukon or the Morrigan lurked without, she'd recognize their foul energy. Delicately, she picked her way through Kheladin's shielding without disturbing its integrity. A stab of joy, so bright it stole her composure, lanced through her. "Witches! 'Tis witches and—"

Mauvreen sidled close. "I do believe you're right, dragon shifter. Witches and my Johnny."

Jealousy bit deep. "Why do ye call him yours?"

A smile wreathed her face. "Don't get your scales ruffled, dragon maid. I stood in for the mother he never had."

CHAPTER 5

*J*onathan's face felt numb, but at least his ears worked again. He'd filled Caty's witches in on everything while one of them patched him up, clucked, and told him he was damned lucky he hadn't lost an eye. The Morrigan had dug her beak in and cut him from orbital socket to jawline, exposing his cheekbone.

"If this doesna hold," the witch cautioned, "ye'll need stitches."

"I'll take magic any day. We've wasted enough time on me."

"Where are you in such an all-fired hurry to get to?" Caty asked.

"I'm going back to Kheladin's cave to raise the alarm, so he and Lachlan can make certain Britta and Tarika are safe." Jonathan bowed formally. "Thank you for heeding my call and helping me." The air shimmered as he summoned magic.

"Not so fast." Caty made a grab for his arm. "If you're off to talk to a dragon, we're coming with you." Her normally taciturn face split into a crooked grin. "We wouldn't miss this opportunity for the world."

Jonathan chuckled. "My coven felt the same way. Open your minds. I'll send you an image of where I'm headed."

He led the group to the entrance point of Kheladin's cave. They hovered outside the most elaborate warding system he'd ever seen. When he'd come through earlier with his coven, the wards had already been down. Ditto for his egress with Britta. Now they formed layer upon layer, wrapped about and pinned to psychic strong points in the ether.

Wow! To have the power to create something this complex, maintain it, and still have energy to play host and chat amiably defies credibility.

What sort of strength did Lachlan possess to bond with such a formidable creature?

His thoughts strayed to Britta, to how her mouth felt beneath his, and his cock sprang to life.

Damn it! Not now.

He buried his libido. It wasn't difficult; he'd had lots of practice. To divert himself, Jonathan focused on the dragon. Kheladin must've sensed the disturbance in his wards. Why hadn't he let them in? Time was critical. It had been at least an hour since the Morrigan vanished, plenty of opportunity for her to go after Britta and Tarika.

Stop! I can't think like that. The dragon is smart. She'd have ferried herself and Britta safely away.

What if they went somewhere I can't follow? Like Fire Mountain? Or hundreds of years back in time?

"Are ye coming?" Someone jostled his arm. He glanced over and saw it was the witch who'd healed him.

"Huh?"

"The wards are dropping. Hurry."

Jonathan squeezed his eyes shut. He'd been so lost in thought, he wasn't paying close attention. He needed to be more on top of things. "Thanks. I'm right behind you."

Kheladin's cave rose around him. Jonathan tumbled out onto its sandy floor. He sprang to his feet and hurtled toward the dragon's bulk. "Kheladin," he shouted. "You've got to make certain Tarika and Britta are safe. The Morrigan—"

Britta—a half-naked Britta—stepped away from a woman with

long, blonde hair and raced toward him. "Thank the goddess ye're unharmed." She stopped a foot in front of him and dropped her gaze. Color rose from her open neckline and turned her face a lovely rose shade.

"I could say the same thing." He closed the distance between them and gathered her into his arms. At first she stiffened, but then she wound her arms around him and hugged him back.

"Ye were a damned fool," she whispered. "A brave one, but a fool nonetheless. Ye might've been killed."

He tightened his hold on her, loving the way her body fit against his. "I could say the same," he countered. "Not about the fool part but about your life being at risk."

"Nay. I am immortal. It comes with the bond to Tarika." She tilted her head back and smiled. "I have a somewhat greater margin for error."

Immortal!

Her lips shimmered tantalizing inches from his. It took all his self-control not to crush his mouth atop hers. "I'd like to hear more about—"

"I dinna think I'd live long enough to see Britta in a man's arms." A tawny-haired man with arresting green eyes draped an arm around each of them. "I'm Lachlan, Laird of Clan Moncrieffe. I'd shake your hand, old chap, but it appears the two of yours are busy."

The blonde, who'd been standing next to Britta, strode to them and placed a hand on Lachlan's shoulder. A knowing smile lit her classic features.

Jonathan's eyes widened. "You're Kheladin's bond partner." He shifted his attention to Maggie. "This must be your wife, er mate."

"Aye. He told you about us, then?" Lachlan grinned. It softened the exacting planes of his face.

"He certainly did. Not just me. All the witches in our coven. I, uh, feel like I should bow or something."

Lachlan cocked his head to one side. "'Twas a time when commoners all bowed to me, but we're far from that era. Power fairly blazes from you. I sense far more than witch blood. In fact, I doona sense witch blood at all. What manner of beings were your parents?"

"Aye," Britta cut in. "I would like to know as well."

"I'm not certain." Three sets of eyes—golden, green, and blue—stared at him. Jonathan swallowed hard. He'd never shared his story with anyone. It was so fantastic, he didn't believe it himself. "I was raised by my father. He and Mauvreen were quite close."

"That would be the witch side," Lachlan cut in. "Or not. As I said a moment ago, I doona sense witch blood in you. Druid mayhap, not witch. Who was your mother?"

Heat rose to Jonathan's face. Britta nestled against his body.

"Whatever 'tis canna be so bad as all that."

"Not bad as much as farfetched. My da was…odd. Touched by the fae. He spun fanciful tales, got lost in prophecies, and never quite found a place for himself in the real world. If it weren't for our coven and the Celtic gods he parlayed with, we'd probably have been reduced to taking public handouts."

"Where is he now?" Lachlan asked.

"I don't know. He left Ireland once I was done with school. I got a job with a software design company and relocated to Inverness a few months before he disappeared."

Mauvreen had approached without him realizing it. "No one asked, but I introduced Caty and her crew to the group here."

"Thanks, but I'm fairly sure most of them already know one another." Jonathan tried to change the subject, but Mauvreen's next words dashed that hope.

"I heard you talking about Angus," she went on. "He was a dreamer. Lachlan guessed correctly about him being a Druid. But there's more. He was a Druidic Seer, who lived in his visions. He could foretell the future with shocking accuracy and sometimes even change it, if he caught something in time. The blood of the Old Ones flowed in him. He never could stand modern life. All those radio waves from wireless routers and phones made his head ache.

As they proliferated, he just sort of faded away, maybe to where the Celts go when they need to find respite."

"Aye, the *Dreaming*." Britta straightened and turned so she faced Mauvreen. "Do ye know who his mother was?"

The witch nodded curtly. "I do, but it's Johnny's call what to say. Even after thirty-five years—"

"Thirty-seven," he muttered.

Mauvreen shrugged. "Little enough difference. You're a man now. You were shamed by your father's oddities as a youth, and you never truly believed the story of your conception and birth, yet they're true."

"How could you possibly know?" Jonathan asked. He'd always sidestepped Mauvreen when she wanted to talk about his origins. Maybe he should've been more aggressive about picking her brain.

"I was there when she brought you to him once you'd been weaned." A half smile softened the planes of her face. "I'd never seen Angus quite so happy. He always wanted a son…" She set her mouth in a hard line. "He wanted your mother too, but she had other priorities." Mauvreen paused, perhaps collecting her thoughts, before adding, "He would've made the effort if your mother was willing. I'm sure of it."

"If ye doona tell me, I'll pluck it from your mind," Britta broke in, her voice sharp.

Mauvreen bristled. Jonathan felt her sheathe herself in power. "Try it, dragon shifter. Some secrets are sacred. Either he will tell you—or not." She turned her whiskey-colored gaze on him. "Your call, Jonathan James Shea."

He squared his shoulders. Maybe the time had come after all. He glanced from Britta to Lachlan to the blonde, Lachlan's mate. Though she hadn't said anything, she watched him intently. He opened his mouth, then shut it again and took a shaky breath. "This isn't going to get any easier. I may as well just spit it out. Arianrhod. My mother was Arianrhod. According to my da, she lay with him in his visions—and after them as well.

"He wouldn't tell me much until I was nearly grown, but then he said they'd made hard decisions about having me and raising me. He —" Jonathan's voice cracked, and he tried again. "He said not to blame Mother, that she did the best she could." He shrugged uncomfortably. "I didn't believe him—about any of it. I figured he was hiding something and made up a story that was so bizarre I wouldn't know where to begin questioning him about it."

Britta inhaled noisily. Lachlan cleared his throat. Jonathan felt like an idiot. They didn't believe him, and he didn't blame them. Who could possibly accept such a tale? He'd never been able to.

"Maybe we could talk about something else," he mumbled. "Like crafting a battle strategy so the Morrigan doesn't catch us unaware again."

"Aye, we need to do that too, but this willna take but a moment." Lachlan closed on him from one side, and Britta twisted in his arms. Each placed a hand on his head.

Jonathan girded himself for blasts of power, but the dragon shifters were gentle. Power crept into him, tentative, exploring. It felt respectful. A look flowed from Britta to Lachlan. They removed their hands. She smiled broadly before stepping away and facing him.

"Aye, 'tis true."

"See." Mauvreen hooked an arm through his. "Told you."

Confusion swept through him, tying his stomach into knots. "All right. Fine. But this doesn't change a thing."

Mauvreen looked down her nose, and he understood. Knowing for sure what and who he was changed everything.

No wonder *I feel so attracted to him. He's one of the gods, or he could be if he let himself believe in his power.*

Britta trained her forthright gaze on him. Jonathan looked as if he'd gone through a war. Resignation replaced disbelief on his handsome face. She saw it in the furrows in his forehead and the lines around his eyes.

"'Twill get better once ye have a wee bit of time to get used to it. Not that ye dinna know afore, but ye paid it no heed." She gripped his hand. "No wonder ye stood up to the Morrigan." A thought surfaced. Britta glanced at Lachlan. "Do ye suppose the Battle Crow knows who he is?"

Lachlan made a rude noise between a snort and a grunt. "I wouldna put it past her. If she dinna afore, now she's tasted his blood, she does. Mayhap she's just as interested in him as you at this point."

"Rhukon seemed thrilled he'd found the two of us." Britta recalled his words. "He said something about a *bonus to boot* after he gloated over finding me."

"None of this is sounding good." Maggie frowned. "Say, would it protect Jonathan if he, um, hooked up with you?" She focused disingenuous blue eyes on Britta. "It already seems you two like one another."

Lachlan elbowed his mate. "Wanting to spread connubial bliss about, lass?"

She grinned. "Aw, gee. Am I that transparent?" All of them turned to her. A chorus of *yeses* and *ayes* rose just before everyone burst into laughter.

"I don't need protection," Jonathan sputtered once the merriment died down.

Lachlan quirked a brow. "Ye lust after Britta."

Color stained Jonathan's face, turning his tanned skin a bronzy gold. "Christ! Are all of you this...frank? It takes more than sex to make a lasting partnership."

Mauvreen horned in. "How would you know? You've been avoiding female entanglements your entire adult life."

Jonathan rolled his eyes. "I don't need Arianrhod to be my mother. You fill the void nicely, *Aunt* Mauvreen."

She cupped a hand to the side of her mouth and leaned forward conspiratorially. "I'm not really his aunt. I'm much too young."

Maggie laid a hand briefly on Jonathan's shoulder. "You're thinking with your twenty-first century mind. If these were normal times and circumstances, of course you'd want to spend much more time courting, getting to know her—"

"Enough." Britta punched a fisted hand in the air for emphasis. She tugged at Jonathan's hand, still encased in hers. "Come. Let's go to where we can have some privacy. Tarika's been giving me hell ever since you told us who your mother was. She wants to talk with you too."

"What about *battle strategy*?" Lachlan mimicked Jonathan's earlier words.

"Honestly!" Maggie dragged him toward where Kheladin held court in the middle of a gaggle of witches. "You're impossible."

"I thought ye appreciated my sense of humor," Lachlan teased, his words fading as he and Maggie walked away.

"I do," she retorted. "But what happened to your sense of romance?"

Lachlan spun Maggie and closed his mouth over hers. Britta knew she was staring, but she felt the intensity of their attraction from thirty paces.

"There." Lachlan lifted his lips from Maggie's. "Enough romance for you, lass?"

"Maybe not." She grinned. "Do it some more."

"They seem happy," Jonathan murmured.

"Aye, that they do. Ready for a bit of conversation?"

He nodded.

"I was just leaving." Mauvreen slipped away.

"Looks as if everyone's left us alone," he noted.

"Aye, but witches and dragons have sharp ears. I'd feel better if we put a wee bit of distance betwixt us and the crowd—and warded our words." She turned and walked toward the sound of running water at the far end of the cave. She was thirsty, plus the waterfall would be an added deterrent in case anyone wanted to listen in. They put a good fifty yards between themselves and the others in the cave. To be on the safe side, she added a bit of magic to mute their words and shield them from prying eyes.

She ducked her cupped hands into the icy pool and drank deeply. Jonathan did the same. Tarika had kept up a running commentary. The dragon liked the idea of them having a mate.

"...And once we've bedded him, we can let Kheladin and Lachlan lead us through the new bonding ceremony."

"Jonathan isna a foregone conclusion." Britta knew her mind voice was snappish, but the dragon's rapid about-face unbalanced her.

"He's practically family," the dragon crowed. *"One of my distant cousins bedded Arianrhod about a thousand years ago."*

"What?" Britta blew out a frustrated breath. *"The supposed virgin goddess fucked everything with a dick?"*

Tarika laughed. *"Hardly. My cousin was verra handsome, black-scaled with blue-green eyes. Almost impossible to resist, though as I recall things, he pursued her—until the Dragon Council put the kibosh on things. It doesna matter. We should make this one ours. I will help with the mating bite."*

"Doona do it yet. He and I must talk."

Jonathan laid a wet hand over hers. "You and Tarika are talking. I sense the energy, but I didn't want to listen in. Would you like me to take a walk and come back in a while?"

Britta shook her head. "Nay. 'Tis ye and I who must figure some things out. Tarika's mind is already made up." She summoned her mage light. Away from the phalanx of witches, the cave was dim. "I know why I've kept to myself. Why have ye not married?"

His throat worked, and he drew his brows together. For a moment, she thought he wouldn't answer, but then he started talking. "Lots of reasons. I was afraid my genetics were flawed." He blew out a breath. "After all, Da was as likely to get lost in a vision state as he was to do anything else. He didn't have much control when they came to him, either."

"Ye're not a virgin," she pressed.

He dropped his gaze. "I suppose you would know things like that. No, I'm not, but for a guy closer to forty than thirty, I've had painfully little experience."

"Why? 'Tis not just ye were worried ye'd produce defective children. There are ways to prevent such things."

"Persistent, aren't you?" His words held a rebuke, but he smiled to counteract it.

She didn't smile back. "'Tisn't easy to become a dragon shifter. I was extremely focused for all the years afore I took myself to Fire Mountain in search of a dragon, and for long years after. I was verra young when Tarika and I bonded, so I had much magical education to make up for, even after we merged." She blew out a breath. "Ye'll just ask me anyway, so I'll save you the trouble by telling you."

"Telling me what?"

"I avoided men for two reasons. No one appealed to me, and they all wanted to control me, to ally with my father's holdings. They saw me as chattel, not a person. I had no interest in any master beyond the magic in my blood, and Tarika wouldn't have stood for it."

"What about other dragon shifters?"

"Such a pairing might've worked, but I never met one I particularly cared for. Humans put land and holdings first. Dragon shifters hold magic dear. Even if I'd found a mage I was attracted to, I would've placed third, right after his dragon and his grimoire. The same would've been true on my side."

Jonathan chuckled. "You shouldn't play second fiddle to anything."

"Thank you. 'Twas the way I saw it." She bowed slightly. "Your turn."

He nodded. "All right. I had a couple girlfriends in high school. Once they came home and met Da, that did it. They ran screaming for the hills. He'd do things like lay his hands on their head and tell them their future—no matter how hideous it was. Of course, everything he said came true, but no sixteen-year-old girl wants to know she'll die of cancer in six years or her parents are having affairs with other people."

"Aye, I can see where it might've been a wee problem." She narrowed her eyes. "'Tis been long years since your da left, why are ye still alone?"

He smiled crookedly. "I've asked myself the same question. Beyond the simple release of sex—and lust became less urgent as I grew older—I guess I never found anyone who pulled my heartstrings—or sang to my soul."

"Och aye, 'tis verra beautiful. Ye spin words like a poet, Jonathan." She cloaked her magic. She could give him the tiniest push but didn't want to. He had to want her for her, not because she'd employed compulsion. She tilted her chin. "What do ye think of me?"

"Truth?"

"Of course." She girded herself to hear him say she was very beautiful, but...

"Ever since I laid eyes on Tarika when you sought help from Kheladin, I haven't been able to think of anything but the two of you. Protecting you from the Morrigan was automatic. I'd have done something, anything, to give you an opportunity to flee to safety. In that moment, I understood I'd lay down my life to preserve yours." He winked lazily. "Of course, I didn't realize you were immortal at the time, but even if I had, I'd still have done the same thing."

Britta swallowed around the lump in her throat. She blinked furiously, her eyes burning with unshed tears. His words touched her heart, but she didn't want to cry. "Thank you."

He speared her with his direct gaze, amber eyes alight with desire and more. A feral protectiveness colored their depths. He took a breath and went on. "I'm so attracted to you, my cock's been hard the whole time we've been together. Even when we were separated, all I had to do was think of you, and I got so hard I ached with wanting you. That hasn't happened to me since I was a teenager."

Britta glanced to where the front of his pants belled out. She wanted to wrap her fingers around his bulge, wanted the cock beneath for her own. Her mouth went dry. Her nipples pebbled into points, and her crotch flooded with moisture. Britta slid Maggie's jacket off her shoulders and tossed her hair out of the way to bare her breasts. Deep in her mind, Tarika cheered her on.

CHAPTER 6

*J*onathan let his gaze rove from Britta's perfect face to her glorious hair and flawless breasts. From there he moved downward to the tangle of red-gold curls in the vee between her legs.

The air around Britta took on a luminous quality, and Tarika's outline formed. *"Ye must want me too,"* the dragon said. Shadowy wings fluttered.

"I do," Jonathan replied. *"You're as amazing as your bondmate."*

The dragon didn't hesitate. Britta's form blurred. Strong jaws closed around the juncture between his neck and shoulder and bit deep. It hurt, but Tarika's bite opened him to the wonder of her mind. Arcane memories crowded behind his eyes, jostling one another for ascendency. Images merged kaleidoscopically, even more compelling than the ones he'd seen when they fought the Morrigan.

"'Tis enough." Britta stood before him again. An indulgent expression softened her beauty, made her more approachable as she undid the buttons on his shirt with nimble fingers. "Tarika was supposed to wait until we mated."

"Not necessarily." The dragon sounded smug. *"If there are rules, show them to me, and I will bite him again if need be."*

"I can hear her without summoning the magic I usually need for telepathic speech."

"Aye, 'tis because she accepted you." Britta snorted. "Ye may wish for the peace and quiet of your own mind afore too long."

"Why would he?" Tarika inquired archly.

Britta pushed at his shirt. He laid his hands over hers. "Wait a minute. I have to unzip the jacket first."

"Unzip?"

He pointed. "Button replacements."

She bent and peered at the metal teeth. "Cunning how they mesh together. When was this invented?"

He slipped his jacket and shirt off his shoulders and dropped them on the cave's sandy floor. His body was electric with arousal. Even the dragon's bite thrummed with unfilled need. "Does it really matter?" His voice rasped with passion, and he held out his arms.

Footsteps pounded toward them. Kheladin surged forward with Lachlan by his side, barreling right through Britta's privacy shielding.

"Excellent." The dragon beamed, double rows of teeth gleaming in the glow from Britta's mage light.

"Yes," Lachlan chimed, sounding excited. "We felt Tarika's mating bite from the far side of the cave."

"And came to congratulate you," Kheladin finished.

"Damn it!" Maggie chugged up behind them. "I told you to at least knock first, or call out, or something."

"Why?" Lachlan stared at her, confusion stamped into his features. "Stop tugging on my arm, lass."

"Even if Tarika bit him, don't you think Jonathan and Britta would like more alone time to enjoy one another?" She elbowed Lachlan. "As I recall, we didn't stop with once."

Jonathan cleared his throat. "We haven't even had *once* yet." He made *go away* motions with both hands.

"Och, sorry." Lachlan backed up a few steps, looking chagrined.

"Aye, sorry indeed. We shall hold those congratulations for a bit," Kheladin seconded.

"How sorry could you be?" Britta eyed Lachlan and the dragon balefully. "You tromped right past my magic to get to us."

"I'm sure I'll be even sorrier once Tarika finishes reprimanding me." Kheladin smirked and turned away.

Maggie blew out a breath. "I had to make love with Ceridwen looking on. The least we can do is give you the illusion of being alone. Here, I'll just add a spot of my own magic to yours." Power thrummed, and she wove a barrier out of golds and greens. The warp and weft joined Britta's spell. Maggie's voice blurred. Jonathan sensed her, Lachlan, and Kheladin leaving.

He shook his head. "Tarika was smart to strike while she had an opportunity."

"A human who understands and appreciates me," the dragon purred.

"Doona encourage her." Britta grinned. "There'll be no living with her."

While he could still think, before the sexual heat thickened so much it addled his brain, Jonathan looked around them. The sandy floor would do, but it would be better if they padded it with their clothing. He bent and arranged his discarded shirt and jacket, and then filched Maggie's jacket from where Britta dropped it.

"Will ye be adding your breeks to the pile?" Britta asked slyly.

"You just want to see me naked."

"Aye, that too."

He toed off his boots and unsnapped his trousers. A quick tug maneuvered the zipper past his hard-on. Britta's voice caught with an audible gasp. She pulled at his pants, clearly anxious to get them out of the way.

"'Twould be far easier if ye wore a plaid." She sounded breathless. "Then we'd simply push it aside."

"Looks as if we managed." He stepped out of his pants and shorts and then kicked them toward the rough bed he'd made. Jonathan placed a hand on either side of her face and tilted it up so she met his gaze. "How would you know about such things?"

"I have eyes. I've watched humans rutting afore. She lifts her skirts, he lifts his plaid. Voila!"

"I don't care about them. I care about us." He traced the bones of her face beneath his fingers. "You're so beautiful. I could look at you forever."

"So are you." She fitted her body to his and wrapped her arms around him. Britta trailed her fingertips down his back. "Your skin is like silk, yet I feel solid strength in the muscles beneath."

He closed his mouth over hers, loving the feel of her lips, firm against his. He licked and nibbled until she opened her mouth to his questing tongue. The same sweet taste as before flooded him. Her hands traveled to his buttocks, and she tightened her hold, fingers digging deep into his muscles. She shifted so she straddled one of his legs, and the heat of her core seared his thigh.

Her scent, heavy with lavender and amber rose around them. He inhaled hungrily, drinking it in, and threaded his fingers into her hair, pulling her more deeply into their kiss. Her hips bucked against his leg. He felt the shudders of a climax ripple through her and held her tight against him until they subsided. One of her hands found its way between their bodies, and she curved her fingers around his cock.

Jonathan broke their kiss, groaning at what her touch did to him. He wanted to toss her onto her back, spread her legs, and bury himself, but he didn't want to hurt her. Dragon shifter or no, she was still a virgin.

"Here." He unwound her fingers from his throbbing cock and gestured for her to lie down.

He joined her on their impromptu bed and strung kisses down her neck to her breasts. Her nipples were peaked. He tongued them, moving from one to the next, while he slid a hand between her legs and rubbed her passion-slick nub until she moaned and writhed beneath his touch. When he knew she was close to another release from the tension in her clit, he moved his hand and pushed a finger inside her. Muscles clenched around him. He added another finger and felt her barrier give way just as the rhythmic contractions of a second climax milked his fingers. He pressed his palm hard against her vulva to make sure she finished. Britta bucked against his hand and shrieked her delight. Her joy warmed his soul. He wanted to make her come a hundred times. A million. He'd devote his life to pleasing her.

Jonathan raised his face from her breasts so he could look at her. Britta's neck was thrown back, corded with passion. Her eyes, shining with heat lust, opened and she met his gaze.

"Ye dinna hurt me." She thrust her hips upward, moving his fingers deeper inside her. She wrapped a hand around his cock and raised an expectant brow. "When do I get the real thing?"

"How about now?" His voice was thick, rough with need.

"Aye, now would be good."

He grinned back. "You're a greedy little thing. You've already come twice."

"Aye. And is there a tariff on orgasms?"

"Not that I've heard of." He tried to move, but she held fast. "You have to let go if you want me inside."

His heart thudded hard against his chest. His throat was so dry he couldn't swallow. He'd never wanted anything as intensely as he wanted the woman splayed before him. Jonathan knelt between her legs and stopped for long moments to absorb her beauty. Taking hold of his cock, he guided the head of it against her opening. He practically came just from the heat of her circling his glans.

She raised her legs and wrapped them around his body, her golden gaze never leaving him. "I'm waiting." She grinned impishly and pushed her hips upward until the tip of him disappeared inside her.

He tried for restraint, lowering himself an inch at a time until the charged warmth of her surrounded him. She wriggled and tightened her muscles until his cock was about to explode. A sweet ache filled his belly, unlike anything he'd felt before. He withdrew and sank inside her twice more before his control fled, and he drove himself into her body faster and faster. Britta gripped his hips. Her nails digging into him only intensified his pleasure.

Heat enveloped him, caught him up, and held him suspended until he felt her pussy contract around him. The climax he'd been holding back blasted out in shuddering bursts of ecstasy. He came for a long time, shattered by the coupling. Gasping, panting, he collapsed atop her and felt her arms close around him.

"'Tis done," she murmured in his ear. "We are joined."

"Aye," Tarika crowed. *"All of us."*

He rolled them onto their sides, pulling her deeper into his arms and making certain he remained inside the silken heat of her body. "You were the most incredible, the most perfect, the most—"

She placed a hand over his mouth. "Hush. Doona ruin it with words."

"Okay. I won't."

Britta snuggled against him. "I'm surprised Kheladin and Lachlan aren't ripping Maggie's spell apart."

"Give them time. They will."

"We need to alter our binding," Tarika nudged.

Jonathan nodded to himself. Yes, there were many things that needed attention. Not the least of which were all the things couples usually worked out before they fell into their marital bed. Like where they'd live and what she'd do while he worked.

"Speaking of bonding." Heat rose to his face. He was glad she was buried in his arms and not looking at him. "Are we, um, married?"

Britta pushed away so she could see him. Her golden eyes gleamed mischievously. "Seems like the sort of question ye might want to have asked afore."

He laughed. "So it is. But I didn't. Are you going to answer me?"

"Would ye like it if we were?" She arched a coy brow.

Well, would I? He considered it. "Yes. Although there are a whole lot of details we haven't talked about at all."

"Such as?"

"Where we'll live. What we'll do. Whether I'll keep working at the same job, although I'll have to work somewhere if we want to eat."

Britta laughed, great rolling gouts of belly mirth. Tears streamed from her eyes. Finally he couldn't stand it.

"What the hell is so funny?" He batted back annoyance. If there was a joke here, it had passed him by.

"Ye just mated with a dragon shifter. Any dragon worth their salt has a hoard. Tarika is ancient, one of the First Born. Ye peeked into her mind. Kheladin's piles of gold pale in comparison to her wealth."

"But that's your money." Jonathan tried for dignity. "I had no idea it existed, probably because Kheladin's the first dragon I ever met and I—"

"Hush. Whether ye work or no is up to you."

"You never answered me about whether we're wed."

"I dinna because the answer depends which set of laws ye pick. If ye choose the covenant that allows dragonshifters to mate with humans, then aye, we are wed since the dragon gifted you with her mating bite. If ye pick common law, then we would need someone to marry us, but if we were together long enough, it wouldna matter."

"If I have a choice, I'll take the covenant and consider us wed."

"Ye're the most wonderful man." She closed her mouth over his and tightened her muscles around his still-hard cock.

Taking it as an invitation, he began a series of long, slow strokes that set his nerves on fire with wanting the woman wrapped in his arms. He'd come once, so he could keep this up forever. She moaned softly through their kiss, and her hips moved of their own accord against him.

"They have to be done fucking by now." Lachlan's voice sounded like it was coming from underwater.

"Maggie and Britta." Kheladin spoke sharply. "Dismantle your combined working, or I'll do it for you."

"Damn! Looks like we're about to have company." Breath ragged, Jonathan withdrew from her body and tugged some of the clothing beneath them into a rough cover.

The magic surrounding them dissipated in multicolored ribbons of light. Lachlan bounded to their side, his nose twitching. "Excellent. I smell sex."

"You're about as subtle as a freight train," Maggie snarked.

"'Tis a good thing I can catch your meaning from context, lass." He turned his attention to Jonathan and Britta. "'Twould be a luxury to leave you the joy of your nuptial bed, but the Morrigan's been battering against Kheladin's wards this past half hour."

Britta pushed to a sit. "Have we time for Tarika and I to separate and re-bond?"

Kheladin stalked near. "Aye, if the Battle Crow could've found her way through, she'd already be here. Only problem is we'll face her the moment we leave."

"Are all the witches still here?" Jonathan asked.

"Up until a few minutes ago." Maggie chortled. "That aunt of yours all but danced a jig once she knew the two of you were, um, intimate."

Lachlan rolled his eyes. "Call a spade a spade, lass. 'Tisn't *intimate*, 'tis fucking."

"You interrupted me," Maggie sputtered.

Lachlan nuzzled her neck. She leaned into him before focusing her gaze on Jonathan and Britta. "Mauvreen wanted to make sure you knew she'd gone back to her house in Fort William. My grandmother's there too. Anyway, she wants the two of you to visit as soon as possible.

Maggie handed Britta a stack of clothes with tennis shoes on top. "These are for you. After we interrupted you the first time, but before the Morrigan showed up, I made a quick trip home, courtesy of an assist from Lachlan's magic, and picked out a few things for you to wear. Shoes, too, though I have no idea if they'll fit."

"Thank you." Britta sorted through the armful, then got to her feet and worked on getting dressed.

Since she wasn't modest in front of the group assembled around their bed, Jonathan took a deep breath and shinnied back into his shorts and pants.

If she can do it, so can I.

He hunted down his boots and tugged them on before getting to his feet. "I'm surprised the other witches left," he said. "Weren't they worried the Morrigan would hassle them?"

"We discussed it," Kheladin rumbled, his voice even deeper than usual. "The tall one ye arrived with left first with two of her witches. The others stood ready to defend them, but it wasna necessary."

"Humph," Britta snapped. "'Twould appear 'tis only dragon shifters—and our mates—that interest the Battle Crow. And mayhap Jonathan on account of his Celtic blood."

Maggie smiled brightly at Jonathan. "How about if you spend some time with me? It'll give the dragons and their bondmates an opportunity to alter the bonding between Britta and Tarika."

Jonathan looked longingly at Britta. He didn't want to let her out of his sight. If there was a place he could take her where the rest of the world would cooperate and fade into non-existence, he'd do it.

"Aye." Britta had clearly been in his mind. "I feel the same, yet both of us are bound by duty as well as our feelings, one for the other. We're just at the barest beginnings, ye and I." She kissed him before following Lachlan and Kheladin.

Jonathan fished his shirt off the floor. He shrugged it on and followed it with his jacket, which he zipped to his chin. Without Britta's warmth, he felt chilled.

"Looks as if the shoes fit," Maggie observed.

"Huh?" Lost in thoughts of Britta, Jonathan didn't follow Maggie's meaning.

"Besotted, aren't you?" She grinned. "Not that I blame you. Lachlan has the same effect on me. If I didn't make a huge effort, he'd be all I ever thought about. I meant the shoes I loaned Britta seem close enough."

He remembered himself. "Thanks for thinking of my...er, mate." Jonathan laughed self-consciously. "Cripes, I don't know what to call her. Girlfriend doesn't do it. She's not exactly my fiancée. She might be my wife, depending on which set of laws I choose to follow." He spread his hands before him, feeling flummoxed.

Maggie skewered him with her gaze, blue eyes alight with humor. "Keep it simple. Focus. We were talking about clothes and shoes fitting."

"Yes." He agreed, grateful to have something manageable to wrap his mind around. "Everything fit fine. Thanks again."

"Much better. It's how I got through the first few days after I met Lachlan. I kept things simple. Or tried to. Dragon shifters can be... intense. Anyway, I brought sweats, a T-shirt, and a stretchy jacket for Britta. So we had a bit of leeway." Maggie squared her shoulders. "Maybe you and I should begin with formal introductions." She extended her hand, and he clasped it. "I'm Margaret Hibbins, but everyone calls me Maggie."

"Jonathan Shea." He opened his senses to her. "You're a witch—a strong one."

"Not so sure about the *strong* part, but I am a witch. Also a doctor."

"Not much difference, really." He let go of her hand.

Maggie snorted. "Yeah, it's what my grandmother always told me. She was annoyed when I went to medical school."

He sucked in a surprised breath as puzzle pieces clicked into place. "You can't be related to *that* Hibbins. Mary Elma, isn't it?"

"'Fraid so. Why am I not surprised you've heard of her?" Maggie cleared her throat. "Everyone has, at least in witchdom."

"Mauvreen, sort of my aunt but not really, knows her from way back. I think they met when she still lived in the States." He shrugged. "Perhaps they were girls together, or something, back in the eighteen hundreds, or maybe the seventeen hundreds. It's hard to get a straight answer out of any of the women about how old they really are."

She smirked. "Isn't it, though?"

He drew his brows together as memories surfaced, "I'm so sorry about what happened to your parents during the last big coven war."

"Yeah, it was pretty awful," she agreed. "That's why I had a sort of love-hate relationship with my magic—until Lachlan showed up, that is."

"How old were you...?" His voice trailed off. It was hard to get the words *when your parents died* past his lips.

"Six. Old enough to understand magic killed them but too young to truly assimilate why." She shook her head, and sadness rolled off her in waves that pricked Jonathan's heart. "I had to blame something for losing them, so I blamed magic. It was only much later I understood they died fighting for something they believed in."

"I wasn't much older than you, but I remember the witches over here talking about it. Your parents were heroes. They kept a sacred formula out of the wrong hands."

Maggie's lips curved into a bittersweet smile. "Thanks. I've never thought of them in quite that light before. It helps."

"You're welcome." He sent healing energy her way.

"Want something to eat?" Maggie changed the subject.

He made a grab for his rucksack and then remembered he'd abandoned it on the streets of Inverness where he met up with Caty and her witches. He'd taken it off to get a drink of water. Between talking with the witches and letting them work on his injuries, he'd forgotten about it—until now. "Yeah, I am hungry, but I left my sandwich a long way from here."

"You're in luck. I brought food back along with those clothes for Britta. Lachlan is always hungry. Dragon shifter metabolism must run at twice the rate ours does."

"After you." Jonathan made a sweeping motion with one hand and followed her.

They sat with their backs against the cave wall. Maggie hadn't been kidding when she said she brought food. He munched on bread and cheese and cold cuts washed down with water from the pool. Maggie was easy to talk with. She fed him questions and answered his. He was beginning to feel drowsy, and wondered how much longer Britta and Tarika would be when a gust of magic rocked him.

Jonathan leapt to his feet with Maggie by his side. His magic collided with hers as they sought the source of the disturbance.

"I think it's okay," she ventured.

"How could it be?" he demanded, his hands raised to summon power. "Whatever's coming is strong enough to blast us to the far reaches of Hell."

"They could, but they won't."

"Goddammit. Who are they?" Every muscle tense, Jonathan balanced power, ready to loose it at a moment's notice. He didn't relish explaining to Lachlan how his mate sustained an injury on his watch.

"Bow to your betters," a deep voice rose from the depths of the cave.

"Ach, those witches never did know their place," a woman retorted.

"I could be mistaken," Maggie murmured, "but I think it's Arawn, Gwydion, and Ceridwen."

"If it is," Jonathan gritted through clenched teeth, "maybe they can take care of the Morrigan. The Celts may have disowned her, but she's still one of them."

Reality slapped him hard. Not only had he actually laid eyes on two dragons, he'd mated himself to a dragon shifter. If Maggie was right, he was about to have a run-in with the Celtic gods. He'd seen them from time to time as a child, but that was long ago. Would they remember him? It might be easier if they did. Perhaps then, they wouldn't look too close and discover the truth about his mother.

A long-buried image of an imposing woman with floor-length silvery hair rose from somewhere. Dressed in form fitting leather, she'd draped a quiver and bow over one broad shoulder. Eyes, one gold and one silver, with the moon reflected in their depths, looked right through him.

Arianrhod.

He'd flouted reality for far too long. She was his mother. No doubt about it.

Maggie raced toward the Celts. Jonathan followed her, but slowly. He needed time to think.

CHAPTER 7

The mage fire enveloping Britta and Tarika receded. The dragon shook herself, and red scales flew every which way. Britta took stock of her body, seeking the new magic that bound her to her dragon. The brief moments after their original bond was severed had been hell. She hadn't truly understood how much a part of her the dragon was until that moment.

"Aye." She tapped her breastbone and blew out a tense breath. "Thanks be to Dewi, our bond is back, right where it belongs."

"Did ye doubt me?" Kheladin sounded annoyed.

Och, best not anger him.

Britta trod carefully. "Nay, but Tarika was old when ye were hatched. Ye said 'twas an arcane spell, which had fallen out of usage, so I dinna understand why she dinna know of it."

"Of course I knew about it." Tarika blew smoke, tinged with gouts of flame, skyward. "Ye were such a courageous maid. I wonder if ye even remember how gutsy ye were when ye traveled alone to Fire Mountain to seek a dragon of your own. Most mages found their dragons on Earth, but not you. Nay, ye had to march straight through the gates of Fire Mountain."

Britta felt heat rise to her face. The dragon had nailed her dead to rights. She'd been young, foolish, impetuous, but most of all, determined. "Aye, but what does my, er, single-mindedness have to do with which spell ye picked to join us?"

Tarika dropped her head low and bent her sinuous neck so she looked into Britta's eyes. "'Twas young ye were. Would ye have been so quick to accept magic that looked different from that which bound the other dragon shifters who trained you?"

Touched, Britta hooded her eyes to shield the emotions churning through her. "Ye wanted me as much as I wanted you."

Kheladin brayed laughter. "Aye, lass, the enchantment that draws a dragon to their mage isna so different from the love Lachlan holds for Maggie." He paused a beat before adding slyly, "Or the love that has taken root in you for the Druid-god, Jonathan Shea."

Tarika spat a glob of fire. It landed close enough to Britta's shoe, it smoked. "Were ye thinking I was just sitting on my scaled haunches waiting for a mage to show up at Fire Mountain and claim me?"

"Er, of course not."

"Good." Tarika straightened to her full, eight foot height. "I knew the minute ye breached the boundaries of our lands we were meant for one another. I dinna say aught, but I was shocked ye were so young, not even twenty as I recall."

"And so ye picked the binding ye thought I would accept," Britta murmured, incredulous she'd been bound to Tarika for hundreds of years, yet knew so little about her.

"Good ye realize it." The dragon had obviously been in her mind. "We shall remedy your lack of knowledge."

"Doona dun yourself," Lachlan said. "I felt much the same once Kheladin and I separated. Like a great dolt for not appreciating—and taking full advantage of—his true potential."

"Why, thank you." Kheladin jammed his snout into Lachlan's back, nearly unbalancing him.

He wound an arm around the dragon's neck. "I admit to more than a few anxious moments since 'twas more than a day afore we re-bonded." Lachlan stroked the dragon's shiny, copper scales. "All the reasons why ye'd wish to remain free tormented me. I had no idea we could share a bond that allowed us both forms."

Britta felt a marked disturbance in the ether—harsh gyrations, where before air had flowed smoothly—and whipped her body to face it. "Magic," she hissed and pointed. "Over there. Someone comes."

"Not possible." Kheladin snorted fire and scented the air.

"Och." A grin split Lachlan's face. "The Celts. Mayhap they've changed their mind about taking care of the Morrigan."

"Not likely," Britta muttered. "They protect their own."

"They should've had a wee bit more problem penetrating my wards," Kheladin groused.

"The Celts were here afore we mated with Maggie. They know the way of your casting. So long as your wards stymied the Morrigan, who cares?" Lachlan sprinted toward the place Britta felt power emerging.

"I care," Kheladin said and stomped after Lachlan's disappearing form. "It means the Morrigan would work her way through eventually. Doona underestimate her."

Britta leaned against Tarika, and the dragon nested her head on Britta's shoulder. She quested for words to tell the dragon how much she loved her for taking a chance on a young, untried mage centuries before, but her tongue felt thick and awkward.

Mayhap 'tis like I told Jonathan about not ruining the moment with words.

"Aye, 'tis exactly the same." Steam plumed from Tarika's nostrils. "Ye needn't say aught. I already know."

"Mayhap we should see exactly who has arrived."

"Sound plan, bondmate. After you."

A thought slammed Britta hard. She muffled a very undignified squeal. "This means I can ride you."

Dragon laughter trumpeted, nearly deafening her. "Aye. Hop on. Ye can practice while we walk across the cave."

Britta chuckled. "Thanks, but I'll wait until we can fly together."

"I'll look forward to it." Tarika nudged her gently with her snout.

Britta watched three Celtic gods emerge from a coruscation in the air, muttering about bowing and witches not knowing their place.

Arawn, god of the dead, shook midnight-dark hair over his shoulders as he clasped Lachlan and Maggie close.

"Move over, ye great oaf. I would hug the lass." Gwydion, master enchanter and warrior magician, elbowed Arawn in the back. Rows of blond braids hugged his head before falling nearly to his waist. Laugh lines in the corners of his blue eyes deepened when he smiled.

"Och, the two of you." Ceridwen laughed long and hard. She was as tall as the men, and her knee-length black hair was shot with silvery-gray. Piercing dark eyes scanned the cave. "Is Arianrhod here? I feel her energy. 'Tis dim, yet I am not mistaken."

"Not Arianrhod but her half-Druid son." Britta stepped forward and bowed low.

Ceridwen sniffed noisily and cackled. "Aye, I smell him on you, dragon shifter. Ye're mated, and newly so if I'm any judge of things. I had no idea Arianrhod had other progeny. Where is this son of hers?"

"Right here." Jonathan trotted out of the shadows and stopped a few paces from the Celts.

Maggie inclined her head toward Ceridwen. "Nice to see you again."

"Aye, ye too, lass."

"Are ye not glad to see Gwydion and me as well?" Arawn trained his dark gaze on Maggie. "Ye hugged us, but ye dinna say aught about—"

"Of course I am," Maggie broke in.

"Och aye." Lachlan threw his hands in the air. "'Tis hardly a social club. Did ye send the Morrigan packing? Surely ye crossed paths with her outside the wards."

Gwydion drew his blond brows together and shook his head. "Donna ye know better than to ask such a question?"

Lachlan let go of Maggie and moved nose-to-nose with the Celt. "Apparently not."

"We never force our own to do aught. It goes against the grain."

"Fine." Britta joined Lachlan. She put her hands on her hips and looked from one Celt to the next. "Then how do you propose we deal with her or the black and red wyverns and their dragon shifter mages? Then there's the little matter of her memory-altering spell. Och aye, but 'tis more than a simple annoyance."

Jonathan spoke up. "If you got rid of the Morrigan, the other dark dragon shifter mages might retreat, along with their dragons."

Britta felt unaccountably pleased when he strode to her side and grasped her hand. She reveled in how solid and comforting and *right* he felt leaned against her, as if he'd always been there. His nearness stirred her in other ways too, and she wished they were still alone.

Britta forced her attention away from the heat building between her thighs. "The only way to get rid of the Battle Crow," she muttered, "would be to engage her in another war. She adores wars —lives for them."

"There's still one going on in the Middle East," Maggie offered.

"Och." Ceridwen rolled her eyes. "'Tisn't big enough to tempt her —not anymore. Besides, she spent years there playing." The goddess adopted a sing-song voice. "Eeny, meeny, miny, moe, who shall be the first to go?"

Britta clapped a hand over her mouth, but she couldn't stifle a startled grunt of laughter. "Sorry," she gasped. "It isn't particularly amusing, but hearing you assign a nursery rhyme to that horror with wings and a beak struck me as funny."

"How about this?" Lachlan tilted his chin upward. "We begin with a clear playing field, which means we get free passage out of Kheladin's cave."

Gwydion cocked his head to one side. He exchanged meaningful glances with Arawn and Ceridwen. "Seems fair enough."

"Ye'll need a more permanent solution," Arawn warned.

"As if I dinna know it," Lachlan snapped.

"I propose a bargain," Britta said in a clear, ringing voice and set her mouth in a determined line. They couldn't kill the Morrigan. The Battle Crow was immortal. They wouldn't even be able to immobilize her—at least not for long.

"We doona bargain with mortals," Ceridwen said. Though her tone was deceptively mild, annoyance threaded beneath it.

"Nonetheless, will you hear me out?" It was tempting to weave compulsion into her words, but Britta feared it would be the kiss of death if the gods had any inkling she'd attempted to influence them.

"What I'd like is to know more about Arianrhod's get." Gwydion stared at Jonathan.

"I'll answer all your questions, so long as you hear my…mate out first."

Arawn chuckled. "Newly mated, indeed. So new, ye doona quite know what to call her."

"My mate just offered a bargain of his own." Britta jumped into the breach. Of course Gwydion would want to know more about Jonathan since Arianrhod was his sister. "What say you?"

"Spit it out, dragon shifter," Ceridwen growled. "We doona like being manipulated."

"I could've tried compulsion, but I dinna." Britta breathed a sigh of relief she hadn't succumbed to the temptation. "What I propose is this. We will find a way to either kill, or otherwise dispose of, the black and red wyverns and their mages."

"While we corral the Morrigan?" Gwydion quirked a brow.

Britta nodded. "And force her to release the memory-altering spell she loosed against dragons. 'Tis a violation of the covenant betwixt you and the dragons," she added archly. "You've been allies since the dawn of time."

"Seems fair enough," Lachlan cut in. "After all—"

"No one asked your opinion," Arawn interrupted, sounding furious.

Britta wasn't surprised. No one liked being backed into a corner, least of all the Celtic gods. She leaned against Jonathan. He was holding his own, and she was proud of him. Beyond that, what an incredible lover he was. Her body still hummed from his touch, and she couldn't wait until they could snatch a few moments alone.

"Mmm... Just what I was thinking."

She wound an arm around his waist and turned to kiss his cheek. *"Ye're eavesdropping on my thoughts."*

"How else will I get to know you better?"

"Touché!"

Faces dark as thunderclouds, the Celts withdrew. They formed a tight circle shrouded by magic so no one could overhear their discussion. Lachlan and Maggie crowded close to Britta and Jonathan, along with the dragons.

"Brilliant," Tarika murmured.

"Aye, wonder if they'll accept the gambit." Lachlan kept his voice low.

"I don't think we need to whisper," Maggie cut in. "The same magic that holds their words secret bars them from ours."

"Good point, lass."

"Aye." Kheladin snorted, bathing them in steam. "'Twas a reason beyond her body ye mated with her."

Maggie glanced up at the dragon. "Thanks...I think."

"While the Celts are busy, I need information," Jonathan said. "Is the reason Gwydion's so interested in me because he and Arianrhod are brother and sister?"

"Probably, though the others are interested as well," Britta answered. "Insofar as they knew, Arianrhod had only two sons, Dylan and Lleu, both conceived by magical means. She's supposed to be a virgin."

"Humph. At least now I understand why she delivered me to Da to raise. I'd have been impossible to explain. Wonder where she hid out while she was pregnant and nursing."

"It wasna all that long." Tarika's scales clattered as she rotated her shoulders. "She could've holed up in a cave those two or three years—or on another world—and not been missed."

"The cat's out of the bag now." Maggie rolled her eyes.

"It certainly is." A corner of Lachlan's mouth turned down. "What do ye suppose will happen?"

Jonathan cocked his head to one side. "If you were right about the Morrigan figuring out who I was, maybe she was planning to, uh, blackmail Arianrhod or something."

"Or use the knowledge as a get-out-of-jail free card," Maggie suggested.

"Huh?" Britta raised a quizzical brow.

"It's a saying," Jonathan explained. "Means she'd use her knowledge as a bargaining chip to avoid having to answer for her execrable behavior when she teamed up with the bad dragons—and their mages."

Lachlan grunted. "Och aye. Maggie called them bad dragons too. They are far more than dragons that have run amok. What is it with you modern humans?"

"Ssht!" Britta pointed. "The Celts are headed our way."

"We've come to a decision," Gwydion announced.

"Aye," Ceridwen broke in. "We shall wait to see how well you do ridding Earth of the black and red wyverns and their dragon shifter mages."

"Once you've accomplished what you can, we shall decide further how to treat with the Morrigan." Gwydion rubbed his hands together.

"She is our kinswoman, after all, no matter what she's done," Arawn added.

"I assume our offer is acceptable." Ceridwen's dark, steely gaze moved among them.

"Why would it be?" Kheladin demanded. "Ye just said ye'll do nothing."

"Not exactly." Ceridwen smiled with all the warmth of a cobra. "We dinna say nay. We said we'd wait and see. Och aye, we will dismantle her memory-jangling spell. The dragon shifter is correct. Such an act is, indeed, a violation of the covenant."

At least 'tis a bit of a concession. Britta drew in a slow breath and blew it back out.

"Seems like a backhanded way to get us to put ourselves at huge risk, possibly for nothing." Jonathan met Ceridwen's gaze.

Britta tugged hard on his arm. *"Doona anger them. They are still gods."*

"Excellent advice, dragon shifter." Gwydion closed on them and focused his intense blue gaze on Jonathan. "'Twould appear ye inherited my sister's stubbornness. I would know how ye came to be."

"I said I'd answer your questions." Jonathan drew himself razor straight, his face cast in stony resolve. "And I will as best I can."

"Did your da make a habit of fucking goddesses?" Gwydion snapped. "Or was it only my sister?"

"I wouldn't have the slightest idea." Jonathan tried to maintain a level tone and remember Gwydion was a god. It wouldn't do any good to snipe back at him.

"And why not?"

"In the first place, I didn't even know what sex was until I was, maybe, ten or eleven. By then, Da had pretty much checked out. His visions became more and more pervasive."

Jonathan shielded his thoughts, though he didn't believe it would do any good. The Celts knew plenty about Angus. They must've realized their incessant demands drove him deeper and deeper into the dream world, but it didn't stop them from piling on the assignments that took Angus away from his son.

What they hadn't figured out yet was that Angus was his da. Maybe if he got really lucky, that choice bit of data would remain hidden.

"Say more." Gwydion gestured with both hands.

"Da was…disconnected from things, including me. Other than

keeping food in the house—and he didn't even do that very well some of the time—it was like living with a ghost."

Gwydion clacked his teeth together. "I canna fathom why my sister would be attracted to a man such as ye describe." He moved next to Jonathan and laid a hand on his head. His touch crackled with magic.

Jonathan ducked out from beneath it, his heart pounding. "What are you doing?"

"Your memory is clouded. Not your doing. Another altered it. Likely my sister. I shall get what I need another way. Doona fear, *nephew*, I willna harm you."

Time passed. Jonathan had no idea how much before Gwydion finally withdrew from his mind. Jonathan puffed out a frustrated breath, still rattled from the forced conversation that wasn't over yet.

Once the Celt accessed Jonathan's memories, the warrior magician grilled him, ferreting out early recollections Jonathan didn't know he still possessed about his time with Arianrhod—and about his da.

Long after Jonathan didn't see how he could possibly dredge up anything else, Gwydion's questions kept coming, and he found himself repeating earlier information.

Britta stood by his side throughout, her arm wrapped around him. A time or two, he felt her ready magic. And he sensed her anger when Gwydion's questioning became truly invasive. No matter how much probing the Celt did, Jonathan had no idea how his da had met the goddess, or how many times they'd lain together.

Finally, Britta made a chopping motion with one hand. "'Tis enough, Gwydion. Ye would squeeze blood from a turnip. He doesna know aught else."

"Aye, unfortunately, ye're probably correct." He turned to Arawn, his face like a thundercloud. "Angus is this one's da."

The god of the dead nodded sourly. "Aye, I figured that out after your trip inside his head. All the while Angus worked for us—or a good part of it, anyway—he carried on a hidden dalliance with your sister. I canna believe he'd be so devious, so disrespectful." A hissing growl blew past his chiseled lips.

"Looks to me like the disrespect ran the other way." Jonathan meant to keep quiet, but the words squawked out of him. "You were the reason Da had such a hard time. You forced him to your bidding, even when he was exhausted and the last thing he needed was one more trip to the dream world. What could you have wanted with my father? He was kind, a gentle soul who—"

"Enough!" Gwydion thundered and slammed the staff clutched in one hand on the cave's floor hard enough sparks flew from its end. "We willna be explaining ourselves to Angus's get."

Arawn looked down his nose at Jonathan. "We remember you well enough."

"Aye." Gwydion turned the word into a snarl. "It took me a while to integrate the child ye were into the man ye've become—even after I plucked the impossible out of your mind. Pfft. Angus told us your mother was a Selkie."

"More fools the two of you." Ceridwen turned on them. "You never thought to check."

"Why was it our job?" Arawn asked coolly. "Ye could've done so yourself—and at any time."

"How dare ye question me?" Ceridwen shook a fist at him.

Angry words swirled around Jonathan. He wanted to ask a million questions because he was still trying to understand what kind of hold the Celtic gods had over his father. Had Angus done something wrong and been forced into servitude?

Britta caught his gaze and shook her head. *"Let them go,"* she sent in shielded telepathic speech.

Arguing like a pack of feral cats, the Celts left as precipitously as they'd arrived.

"Wonder if they'll still ride herd on the Morrigan so we can leave?" Jonathan mused. Worrying about logistics was easier than puzzling over what the Celts wanted with his father.

"'Tisn't as if we couldna fight our way out," Lachlan muttered.

"Aye," Britta concurred. "Six against one—even when that one is the Morrigan—are decent odds."

"We have no idea where the black and red wyverns are—or their mages," Tarika reminded them.

"Och." Britta nodded. "Quite the oversight on our part, eh?"

"Ye might say so." Tarika sounded smug.

"Where are we going?" Jonathan asked. Kheladin and Tarika were eminently likeable, yet fierce at the same time.

Glad they're on our side, even if they do like to indulge in saying I told you so.

"Good question." Maggie pursed her lips. "Where do you live?"

"I have a flat here in Inverness, very close to the town center."

"Mauvreen and Gran are in Fort William at Mauvreen's. I know they want us to join them." She dragged a cell phone out of a pocket, looked at it, and grimaced. "Five a.m. No wonder I'm beat."

Jonathan didn't have to dig very deep to realize he was desperate for some private time with his new mate. "I'd like to bring Britta to my house, at least for a little while. We'll take care to ward it."

"Let's do this," Kheladin suggested. "Tarika and I will join Mauvreen and Mary Elma in Fort William. You four show up this evening, and then we'll strategize."

Maggie laughed. "By then my grandmother will already have a plan firmly in place."

"If we doona agree, we'll craft something different." Britta shrugged. "Majority rule."

"Best of luck. Gran's her own majority and pretty stubborn. Um, do you actually think the Celts will do anything about the Morrigan?" Maggie asked pointedly. "Seems to me this is just a roundabout way of suckering us into helping them out."

"What would ye have us do?" Britta caught Maggie's gaze and held it.

A sheepish grin spread over her face. "Good point. I guess we'd go after Rhukon, Connor, and their dragons, no matter what the Celts told us."

"Aye." Britta agreed. "Even if they do nothing about the Morrigan, if we can cut the knees from beneath her subordinates, we'll dilute her chokehold on Earth."

"This conversation is in danger of becoming circular." Lachlan winked lewdly. "I propose we regroup tomorrow morning. 'Tisn't as if Maggie and I have had much time to enjoy one another, either."

"'Twill feel strange to be separated from Tarika for any time at all," Britta murmured and walked to the dragon's side. "Shall we gather in Fort William this evening? 'Twill give us the whole of the day with our new mates."

"Aye, it does feel odd to have the dragon apart from you," Lachlan said, "but ye'll feel the bond, no matter how far away ye are, one from the other."

"If you're lonely for Tarika," Jonathan moved to Britta, capturing her between his body and the dragon's side, "we can join her in Fort William whenever you want."

"Thank you." Britta hugged him. "There is much here that's new. 'Twill take getting used to."

You're not kidding. Dragons, gods, the Morrigan, being as good as married, the Celts using Da for goddess only knew what...

"I doona know about the rest of you," Lachlan said, "but I'm thinking we should leave while we can, without having a direct confrontation with the Crow."

"Agreed." Britta untangled herself from Jonathan and opened her arms to Tarika. The dragon bent low and bathed everyone in a blast of steam. "I love you," Britta murmured. "We'll meet again verra soon."

"Count on it." The dragon shut one scaled eyelid in a parody of a wink.

"I'll take good care of her," Kheladin promised and shuffled close. "Link to my mind, Tarika. I know where we're bound." The air took on a shimmery aspect, and the dragons vanished.

Britta laid a hand over her chest. Sensing her uncertainty at being separated from Tarika, Jonathan gathered her close. He glanced at Lachlan and Maggie. "I know where Mauvreen's is. We'll see you there before too long."

"Even if ye dinna know, I can always find Tarika." Britta spoke softly against his shoulder.

Now why didn't I think of that?

"You're not the only one dealing with new things," he said. "Of course you could find Tarika through your bond. I feel like an idiot."

"I dinna mean—"

"Ssht." He kissed her hair. "No offense taken."

"We're leaving," Maggie announced. "Britta, would you like me to bring a few more clothes to Mauvreen's since everything of mine fits you?"

Britta moved out of the circle of Jonathan's arms. "Aye. If it wouldna be too much trouble, I'd dearly appreciate the kindness." A smile lit her eyes, and burnished copper flecks warmed their golden hue.

"Consider it done."

Jonathan felt the sting of magic, smelled its sharp scent—lemony with a petroleum undercurrent. In seconds, Lachlan and Maggie were gone.

"Shall we follow them?"

"Will ye send me an image of where we're going?"

"I'll do you one better. I'll take us there. Ready?"

She squared her shoulders and nodded. He thought about the best place to bring them out and targeted his living room. He hadn't thought to ward his home before leaving, so there was always the slightest chance one of the wyverns—he still wanted to call them bad dragons—might be waiting for them, along with their mages.

Not much I can do about it. If I aim for another location, we'll risk exposure when we walk to my flat.

He girded himself for combat. His virtual gaming world had come alive, and he felt woefully unprepared. At least they were still solidly within the hour the Celts had promised, so the Morrigan shouldn't be an immediate problem—assuming she honored her kinfolks' wishes. He still couldn't believe the revelations about his father. The Celts talked about him as if he'd been some sort of indentured servant. Who knew? Maybe he was.

Britta shivered. Apparently, she'd been in his mind. "I'm sorry ye found out those things about your da, and I've always hated the Crow."

"It'll take some time—and a bunch more information—for me to understand why Da worked for them and put up with all their shit." He inhaled raggedly. "I know the reasons I hate the Morrigan, but why do you?"

"Ye should see her on the field of battle, blood streaming from her beak and feathers. She glories in death. 'Tisn't natural."

"If luck is with us, we won't have to think of anything but one another for at least a little while." Jonathan held out his arms. She walked into them, and he summoned the magic to transport them from the dragon's cave.

Britta inhaled deeply and then did it again. Jonathan's scent brought a smile to her face and made her feel all melty inside. He smelled heavenly, like musk and bay leaves, with a sweet cinnamon edge. She burrowed deeper into his arms. Not having Tarika by her side felt strange, as if she were missing a limb. Lachlan had been right—she sensed the bond, yet she missed the dragon's presence.

'Tis all for the good. We will be far stronger with the current binding because we can fight as separate entities.

Och aye, I can reason with myself all I want. The long and short of it is, I miss her.

From what she'd seen of modern buildings, none were large enough to accommodate Tarika, but the dragon could still fold herself within Britta, just as they'd done before.

Aye, and 'twill work the other way too.

The blackness surrounding them faded. Britta blinked as a room took form. A room that smelled just like the man holding her. She readied magic in case, but nothing threatened them. Britta wriggled in Jonathan's arms. Craning her neck, she gazed at an oblong space with leather furniture and polished wooden floors. The walls were lined with overflowing bookshelves. Things she didn't recognize sat on tables.

"You miss her, don't you?" Jonathan asked. "Your mind's been busy, but I've stayed out of it to give you privacy."

Britta leaned back and looked at him. "Ye needna do so. After all, we're mated and shouldna hold secrets. Aye, I do miss Tarika. 'Tis worse than I imagined, yet not so bad I canna stand it."

He tilted her chin with a finger and held her gaze. "If you want, we can draw more magic. Just say the word. Next stop could be Fort William and Mauvreen's house."

She narrowed her eyes, considering. "Nay. I've had centuries to build what's between Tarika and me. Ye and I need time as well."

A heartfelt smile blazed from his eyes and illuminated the striking bone structure of his face. She knew he made the offer because he cared about her but was relieved she chose to remain just the two of them.

"Give me a moment to ward the place." His power surged, and she joined hers to it. The two together would make stronger shielding. His smile morphed into a grin. "Thanks. I'm not used to working with anyone else, but I see the advantages. Can I offer you something to drink or eat?"

"Aye, but first, tell me what that black box is just there. And the other, which looks a bit like it, on the far side of the room."

"The first is a computer monitor. What powers it is beneath the desk. The other screen is a television."

"Computers. Isna that what ye design or build?"

He took her hand and pulled her gently toward an elaborately carved desk made of dark wood. Kneeling, he tapped a box she hadn't seen. "This is a central processing unit. It has a circuit board inside that determines how the computer does things. I design circuit boards. They're kind of like electronic brains."

She knelt next to him and ran her hands over the box. "Open it," she demanded. "I wish to see." He unclipped metal latches and lifted one side of the box away. The thing whirred to life, ablaze with small lights.

"Och." She drew back. "What manner of arcane magic is this?"

"Sometimes it feels like magic run amok when things aren't going well, but it's just a bunch of circuits operated by logic. The only time magic ever comes into play is when I curse the damned thing."

She snorted. "I need a dictionary to talk with you."

He punched a cunningly recessed black button, and the box quieted. "Come on." He straightened and helped her up. "I have a better idea. Let's have something to eat and drink and then—"

"Drink, aye. Let us toast our mating. I doona wish to waste time eating. The witches will have food once we get to Fort William." She inhaled sharply. "We doona have much time, and I'd rather spend it making love, getting used to one another."

"A woman after my own heart."

He stepped around her and pulled a bottle of spirits and two shot glasses from a cupboard. Filling the glasses, he handed her one and clinked his against it. "To us."

"Aye, to the love that will grow between us." She tipped her glass back and drank. Whiskey burned as it traveled down her throat to her stomach.

He set his empty glass on a side table and focused his amber gaze on her. "What you said about getting used to each other...I never want to get too used to you." The heat of his need pierced her from where he stood. "I've held this sense of awe, of wonder, ever since you invited me into your body. If I could, I'd hang onto it forever."

"Aye, the soul of a poet." She placed her glass next to his, then closed the short distance between them and opened her arms. He wound his around her and kissed her, tongue probing, teeth nipping. A jolt of sexual yearning zapped her. The clothes between them were first an impediment and then an annoyance as she struggled with unfamiliar fastenings.

"Let me." He undid whatever held her breeks in place. She pushed them down her hips, and they tangled in her shoes. "Hold on." He scooped her into his arms as if she weighed nothing and walked to the far end of the room, then down a short hallway and through another door.

His bedchamber. Tall dressers made of light-colored wood graced two walls. Another computer monitor, twin to the one she'd seen in the living room, sat atop a small table with one chair. Papers were piled high on the table, but the rest of the room wasn't cluttered. He laid her on the bed and bent to remove her shoes. Once they were out of the way, he pulled her breeks the rest of the way off.

"I can't believe how stunning you are." He ran his hands the length of her body almost reverently.

"Ye still have your clothes on." Her mouth was so dry, it was hard to get words out.

"So I do." He sat on the edge of the bed, his gaze never leaving her, and removed his boots. They made little clunking noises as they hit the floor. He stood and undid his breeks, stepping out of them. His smallclothes followed.

She motioned with one hand, and her mage light flared into brightness. "I would see you, all of you."

He dropped his jacket over a chair, then unbuttoned his shirt and slid it off his shoulders. Britta had to remind herself to breathe. He had the most incredible body with dusky, golden skin that gleamed in the glow from her light. Well-muscled shoulders and legs, slender hips, and a sprinkling of dark hair around copper-colored nipples captivated her. His flat stomach was corded with muscle. Jutting out from his body, his cock twitched, hard and ready, heavy with need. He unbraided his hair. Freed, the dark strands fell halfway to his waist.

"I canna stand the distance between us." She patted the bed next to her and pushed the covers back.

He smiled crookedly. "You still have your shirt on."

Britta tugged off her jacket and pulled the stretchy shirt over her head. Her breasts ached, the nipples hard points of desire. "If ye doona come to me, I'll—"

He was by her side in a trice, tracing one erect nipple with a fingertip. "You'll what?"

She opened her arms, too overcome with desire to speak.

CHAPTER 9

*H*er arousal ignited his own, like tinder to flame. Not that his needed a boost. The way things were looking, he'd be lucky not to come before he even got inside her. Lavender, amber, and musk tickled his nose. The hotter she got, the more intense her scent became. It surrounded him, almost like a living creature, caressing his soul. He gazed at her, still unable to believe she was his. What a breathtaking woman. He fitted his body to hers and kissed her, tasting the single malt Scotch they'd drunk. She wove her arms around his back and buried her hands in his hair. Her body writhed beneath him as she captured one of his legs between hers and pressed the hot wetness of her core against his thigh.

Her full breasts strained against him. He sank his tongue into her mouth, and she wound her fingers tighter into his hair. He'd never kissed anyone like this before, where the only thing in the world was the taste of her lips against his, the sweet warmth of her mouth and tongue. He rolled her onto her back. She moved her legs up and back, and then circled his waist. He wanted to do so many things: kiss her, suckle her nipples, move lower and taste her musky center, but his cock had a mind of its own. Once she opened her legs, it seated itself in her opening. Still, he tried to hold back, to savor the incredible hunger coursing through him, setting fire to every nerve ending.

Her hips heaved and rolled beneath him. Britta ran her hands down his back until they settled on his ass. She gripped him and pulled hard. He held fast. Once the magic that was her pussy encased him, he'd come. She broke their kiss and nipped his lower lip. "I'm going to spend. I would do so with you inside me." Her voice was husky with passion.

Inch-by-inch, he lowered himself into her, riding a ragged edge of control. He was damned if he wouldn't last long enough for her to come at least once. Jonathan withdrew until just his cockhead danced around her entrance. At the bottom of his third full stroke, her muscles clenched again and again. She cried out in Gaelic and clawed his back.

His balls snugged against his body and control fled, blown away like so much fairy dust. He balanced on his arms so he could look at her beautiful, passion-splotched face and breasts and withdrew, but not all the way. Because he couldn't wait any longer, Jonathan drove himself into her again and again. The orgasm he'd ridden herd on was so close his balls ached. Finally, he couldn't stand any more sensation and juddered hard inside her. Semen burned as it burst from his body in gouts of pleasure so intense his vision grayed at the edges.

She gripped his hips and ground herself against the base of his cock. "Aye," she moaned. "Again."

Her legs tightened around him, and he willed himself to keep moving until after a second climax rippled through her, and the tension in her muscles relaxed. He lowered his body atop hers, murmuring endearments and covering her face and neck with kisses, overcome by the intensity they'd shared.

Jonathan learned to keep a firm grip on his emotions as a young teen. It served him well as a survival skill because his father wasn't available in the sense most parents probably were for their children.

The visions had intensified, and Angus couldn't help his absences, but they left Jonathan with no one to turn to at a time when he was figuring out what it meant to be a man.

Britta blew the lid off his carefully crafted emotional detachment. He wanted to hold her, care for her, protect her from harm, watch her belly swell with their children…

"Och aye, and I would be wanting those things as well." She smiled and rolled from beneath him so they lay side-by-side.

Heat rose to his face. "I guess you were inside my head."

"Of course. Isna that what lovers do? Share each other's innermost thoughts?"

"Sure, but I was raised in an era where we use words for that."

She arched a brow. "Would ye prefer I stayed out of your mind, then?"

Jonathan thought about it. "No. I want just what we have." He cupped the side of her face with his hand. "I have no secrets from you."

"Good. 'Tis the way things should be." She snuggled deeper into his arms.

"How would you know the way things ought to be?" he teased.

"I may have been unmated, but I have eyes and ears."

Her breathing settled into a regular pattern. He cradled her against him, knowing he should sleep too, but the wonder of her in his arms kept him awake. From confirmed loner to sharing his life with a woman and her dragon was quite a shift. Despite not knowing Britta for long, he couldn't imagine not having her by his side. He looked forward to getting to know Tarika too. That she and Britta had maintained independent personalities over their long years of linkage amazed him.

His thoughts strayed to his da. The Celts had utilized his seer ability in some capacity for reasons Jonathan could only guess at. Surely they had their own seers, Bran for one. Jonathan pressed his lips together, feeling frustrated. There was no way to untangle that particular mystery without access to his da, something unlikely to happen—at least anytime soon. Angus was well and truly gone from the British Isles. Jonathan had spent enough time looking for him to understand there wasn't any point expending further effort along those lines.

Not much he could do about Angus, so he shifted to considering the danger they faced. Somehow, he didn't believe the Morrigan or the red and black wyverns—and their dragon shifter mages—would ever roll over on their backs and say *I surrender.*

"Of course they willna do any such thing," Britta said, her voice fuzzed with weariness.

"Hush." He stroked her hair back from her forehead and tangled his fingers in its silky strands. "Go back to sleep."

"There are times for such things. Now isna one of them." Sandwiched between their bodies, his cock stirred to life. She butted her pelvis against it. "I know I said we could wait to eat, but I would welcome a bit of a meal along with another jot of whiskey."

His stomach growled in agreement, making him laugh. "Pitched battle between body parts. My stomach wants food. My cock wants more of you."

She slipped a hand between them and curled her fingers around his shaft. "Food for the body now. Food for our love later."

"Looks like I'm not the only one with a poet's soul." He nuzzled her neck. "Can I get you a robe? I have an extra one."

She nodded. He got to his feet and plucked both bathrobes off hooks behind the door. She padded next to him, and he helped her into a soft, blue terrycloth robe before snugging the striped one around himself. "What do you feel like eating?"

Britta shrugged. "I'm not familiar enough with food in this time. Anything would be fine. Bread. Cheese. Meat."

"Soup?"

"Doona ye have to cook that for hours?"

"It comes in a can now, but you can still make it from scratch if you have time."

She drew her blonde brows together. "What do ye mean *in a can?*"

"Come along. I'll show you."

He settled her at his small kitchen table and opened a can of chicken noodle soup. Next he got bread out of the refrigerator and made them tuna sandwiches while the soup heated.

She turned the aluminum soup can around in her hands. "Is there other food that comes this way?"

He tapped the empty tuna can on the counter with a fingernail. "You can get most anything in tins."

"Why doesna it spoil?"

"Good question. Early on in the canning process, people died from eating food in tins that hadn't been adequately cooked, but it's not a problem anymore. Basically, what's in the can is processed with heat and pressure until all the bacteria—er, little bugs—that might make you sick are dead."

Britta wrinkled her nose. "Ewww. It seems fresher food would still be better."

"That's the party line." He set a plate and bowl in front of her. "But I'm a confirmed bachelor. We're notorious for our poor eating habits."

"Ye'll have to explain *party line.* I got the other part. Ye need a mate to see ye eat better. Men havena changed overmuch since the Greeks." She took a sip of soup and frowned. "It doesna taste like much of anything."

Concern smote him. His slipshod eating habits might not work for Britta. He hovered halfway between counter and table, his own dishes in hand. "Would you like to get dressed and go out? We could find something better."

"Nay." She took a bite of sandwich, then chewed and swallowed. "I appreciate ye made me a meal. Now, if we could chase it with a bit of spirits, all would be well."

"Is the scotch all right or would you prefer ale?"

"Scotch."

He poured the liquor, added a bit of water to his, and sat across from Britta where he could drink her in. "It's such a wonder to have you at my table, to share a meal with you…" His voice trailed off. He felt awkward, like an adolescent on his first date.

"I feel the same way." She lifted her glass. "To us."

He clinked glasses. "To us. And to victory so we have long years to enjoy each other."

"Aye. I'll drink to that as well."

They ate in silence for a few minutes. It felt companionable, domestic, things he'd never expected to find for himself. "I know enough about the Morrigan. Maybe you could tell me about the black and red dragons. All I know is they're dragon shifters like you and Lachlan."

She met his gaze, her golden eyes serious. "Aye. Rhukon is the black wyvern's mage."

"His dragon's name?"

"Malik." She hesitated. "His defection is hard for me since he and Tarika were egg-mates millennia ago."

Jonathan racked his brain for what he knew about dragons, which wasn't much. "Do you mean they came from the same clutch?"

"Aye. They shared a mother but obviously had different fathers. 'Tis why Tarika is called First Born, while he is not. Tarika's father was one of the first dragons to be formed deep in the maw of Fire Mountain."

"So not just different colors but different bloodlines," Jonathan murmured. Britta nodded. "How long have Rhukon and Malik been bonded?"

She cocked her head to one side. "I'm not entirely certain, only that it happened after Tarika and I chose one another."

"And the red wyvern?"

"Aye. The mage is named Connor and the dragon, Preki." Responding to the question in his eyes for more information, she shook her head. "I doona know much of either. Connor's magic isna particularly strong. 'Twas a surprise to all of us when he bonded with a dragon at all."

Jonathan grappled for food on his plate and realized he'd finished his sandwich. "I'm going to make myself another. Would you like more?"

Britta raked her hair away from her face and pushed it over her shoulders. "Doona think me ungrateful, but have ye aught that isna in a tin?"

He grinned. "How about a toasted cheese sandwich?"

"Hot cheese and bread?"

"Yup."

"I can make it if ye show me where things are."

He held up a hand. "Nah. Even my limited culinary arts can turn out toasted cheese sandwiches." He rustled in the refrigerator and found a chunk of cheddar, before pulling a cast iron skillet from a cupboard.

She sipped her scotch and watched him. "What happened to the serving classes who used to take care of housecare and cooking?"

"People who have lots of money still employ domestic help. The rest of us make do." He flipped a sandwich onto a fresh plate and walked it to her. Because it looked better than a second go-round with tuna and mayonnaise, he made himself one as well. She was half done with hers before he got back to the table. He grinned. "Better?"

"Aye." She grinned back. "Much. At least this bears a passing resemblance to food. Are ye feeling more balanced about your da?"

He took a bite, savoring the melted cheese and crisp bread. "Not really, but there's nothing I can do about it, so I'm focusing on other things. Do you know how the Morrigan and the two wyverns got together?"

"That I do." She poured another half finger of scotch into her glass. "'Twas during one of those interminable battles that peppered the old country in the fifteen and sixteen hundreds. The Morrigan was in her element. She solicited recruits to help manage the dead."

"Er, this may be a stupid question, but why wouldn't she have teamed up with Arawn, Celtic god of the dead?"

"She did, until Arawn grew sick of her. What I meant to say was she got Rhukon and Connor to talk people into changing sides afore they actually died." Britta rolled her shoulders. Jonathan jumped to his feet. He came around behind her and massaged the sides of her neck. "Och, but your touch feels heavenly." She leaned into his hands.

"Originally, you said *manage the dead*."

"So I did. See, it dinna matter which side the poor sods fought on. Most of them died anyway. But it helped the Morrigan's cause if the proper side was victorious because it meant war would continue." She laid her hands atop his. "Finish your meal while 'tis still warm."

He returned to his seat and addressed the remaining half-sandwich, consuming it in just a few bites. "Let's see if I have this straight. The Morrigan used Connor and Rhukon to solicit cooperation from men fighting on the side she wanted to lose." At Britta's nod, he went on. "Why'd they stick with her after the fighting was done?"

"She may have promised to find them dragons to bond with. For a brief time, dragons liked the Battle Crow, and she enjoyed the adulation. Most of the Celtic gods always looked down on the Morrigan. They allowed her to be one of them but in a bit of an inferior capacity. I doona know for certain, but I believe she kept dragons close to boost her sense of self-importance."

"After hundreds of years, the partnership just sort of stuck," Jonathan murmured half to himself.

"Nay, not exactly. Most dragonkind saw through her fairly quickly, but the easily corruptible ones remained her allies."

"Evil's always attracted its like. Had enough to eat?"

"What else have ye?"

He remembered Belgian chocolates tucked away in a high

cupboard and got the box. "Here." He opened it and set it on the table. "Sweets."

She plucked one from its fluted paper cup and popped it into her mouth. The amazed expression on her face almost made him laugh. Clearly, she hadn't been expecting the rich confection.

"Mmmm. Wonderful," she said once she could talk, and grabbed another.

"Yes. They are. Mauvreen knows I like them, so she brings them to me." He picked a piece he knew had cordial inside.

"Mauvreen's been around your whole life, but she talks differently. Now I think about it, she sounds a lot like Lachlan's mate."

"Because both of them are from the States."

"Which states?"

"The New World?"

"Och, aye. Across the great ocean."

He nodded. "Mauvreen's been here for, maybe, fifty years. But she still sounds like the New Yorker she started out as." Britta looked confused, so he hurried on. "New York is one of fifty United States, but none of that is especially important."

"Nay, 'tisn't. I'll have years to catch up on modern history. We're done feeding our bodies," she noted coyly.

"Maybe I can really make love with you this time." His cock stirred, hardening against his upper leg. "We can start in the bathtub. I'll wash your body and your hair and then we'll—"

"Doona be telling me. Show me." She laid the heels of her hands on the table and got to her feet. Her robe puddled on the floor after she slid it off her shoulders.

He tossed his robe over hers and wound his arms around her. Glorying in the feel of her in his arms, he crushed his mouth down on hers. Despite their earlier lovemaking, need was sharp and so urgent it stole his breath. He ran his hands down her back and gripped the globes of her ass, lifting her easily onto his erection.

Britta wrapped her legs around his hips, her arms around his shoulders, and tightened her pussy muscles around him. She tore her mouth from beneath his. "Bath," she rasped, smiling like a mischievous imp. "I thought ye said the first thing was a bath."

"Do you want to stop?" He thrust his hips upward, burying himself to the hilt.

"Nay." She threw back her head, neck corded with lust, and laughed. "I want you to fuck me. Fast and hard. The bath can wait."

"Remember," he growled. "You asked for this." He slid his forearms beneath her buttocks to balance her weight better and moved his cock in little tantalizing circles inside her.

"Oooch." She writhed against him, pushing her clit against his pubic bone. "Close." She turned passion-swollen lips up for more kisses. Soon after he closed his mouth over hers, he felt the rhythmic contractions of her release. Maybe it was the decadence of their position or her unbridled lust, but he couldn't hold himself back. As soon as he felt her coming, his own climax found its way to the surface. He came hard, shuddering over and over and crying her name.

"Aye, beloved," she murmured once his body stilled. "'Twas what ye called me. Beloved. I think I rather like it."

Heart thudding so hard it was a struggle to breathe, he relaxed into their embrace. "About that bath..."

"Och aye." She wrinkled her nose. "Now we need it more than ever."

CHAPTER 10

A Few Hours Earlier

Kheladin drew Tarika close and summoned magic to transport them to Fort William. "What think ye of the new bond?" The walls of his cave disappeared beneath them.

"It feels…strange. I've been linked, talon and claw, to Britta for so long, it feels as if part of me is missing." She blew a plume of smoke. "What's even stranger, though, is her fascination with Jonathan. Not that I'm not pleased by the turn of events, mind ye, but I thought sure she'd be a maid forever."

"'Tis far more than infatuation," Kheladin informed her. "It has the feel of Lachlan and Maggie's bond."

"Aye, ye're right about that, which is why I bit him to formalize their mating."

Kheladin chuckled. "Aye, and ye dinna wish to risk Britta changing her mind."

"Mayhap that too. 'Tis a good thing he makes her happy. When I met Britta, she was an overly serious maid, and she grew into a woman with grim edges."

"All dragon shifters are dour at times," Kheladin concurred. "'Tis because they forego much to be bonded to us."

Scales rattled as Tarika shook herself. "I miss flying places. Having to be shrouded in magic is trying. 'Tisn't far from Inverness to where we're going. We could take to the skies and—"

"I havena been here long," Kheladin cut in, "but there are no dragons, except for us, that is."

"So?"

"Maggie says modern people have weapons that could shoot us out of the skies."

"We're immortal, or have ye forgotten?"

"Nay. I havena forgotten, but it could take long years to repair our bodies if they are too badly broken."

"And we must save our strength for the battle that matters. Doona mind me. I stayed too long at Fire Mountain and in an earlier era here on Earth. 'Twill take a wee bit of time afore I'm familiar with the realities of living in this world."

"Let us hope the world remains intact long enough for ye to get your wish."

"Do ye believe straits are so dire?" Tarika asked.

"Aye, but doona take my word for it. Ye can speak with Maggie's grandmother and Mauvreen, two powerful witches."

"Aye, I met the one. A wee bit on the overbearing side."

Kheladin laughed. "Wait till ye meet Mary Elma. She makes Mauvreen look like a piker. It willna be long, we're nearly there."

He brought them down in the warded yard outside Mauvreen's house. The witches must've been expecting them because they sat on the bottom porch step, mugs of something that smelled alcoholic in hand.

Mary Elma sprang to her feet and trotted toward them. "Where's that granddaughter of mine? And her consort."

Kheladin blew a plume of smoke skyward. "I'm thinking Lachlan might see Maggie as *his* consort, but it doesna make all that much difference. They are at her home in Inverness—"

"—fucking each other's brains out." Mary Elma rolled her dark eyes and raked her hands through long, black hair flecked with gray.

Her black skirt brushed the ground, and a long black tunic encased her wraith-thin upper body.

"Don't be hard on them." Mauvreen came forward. "They've only just discovered one another. I remember what it was like to be young."

"Do you now?" Mary Elma turned a sour expression on her friend. "Maybe I'm just too old and withered to remember the feel of a man's cock—"

"Bullshit!" Mauvreen said succinctly. "Just last Beltane, you had so many men, I was a bit jealous. At one point, they were lined up to sample you."

Mary Elma's alabaster complexion turned the color of fresh blood. "Humph. I'd forgotten you were there."

Mauvreen shot her a triumphant smile. "You might borrow a page from my book. I'm not begrudging Johnny a minute he can steal with his dragon shifter, not when he's finally met a woman who's worthy of him."

"You always sounded more like his mother than anything else," Mary Elma huffed.

"And why not? The poor boy never had a mother."

"Of course he did. She just didn't want to blow her cover as a virgin goddess. Enough of this." Mary Elma walked around Kheladin to Tarika and stared up. "I suppose your mage is the one who's taken up with Jonathan?"

Tarika exchanged glances with Kheladin. He shook his head almost imperceptibly, hoping she wouldn't antagonize Mary Elma. Tarika exhaled steam.

"Aye, ye'd be correct." She inclined her head toward Mary Elma. "Ye must forgive me. I'm not used to such things being bandied about quite so openly."

"Maybe they'd like something to eat?" Mauvreen suggested cheerily.

Kheladin brightened. "Is there a forested area nearby where we might hunt?"

Mary Elma joined her friend and poked her. "What were you thinking of offering them? Watercress sandwiches?"

"For the love of Pete, Mary. Give it a rest." Mauvreen blew out an annoyed-sounding breath. "I was just trying to be a good hostess. If what they need is a cow or sheep, there's not much I can do about it."

"I'm sure we'll be fine," Tarika said hastily. "Mayhap we could use this time afore our bondmates return for you to catch me up—and Kheladin, too, though he's had greater opportunity than me to accustom himself to how things are now."

"What would you like to know?" Mary Elma sank onto the grass in a cross-legged sit.

Tarika and Kheladin lay on their bellies, snouts at ground level, one on either side of Mary Elma.

"I'll just refresh our drinks." Mauvreen plucked the mug from Mary Elma's hand and strode into the house.

Kheladin considered the witch's question. "For starters, did ye realize the Morrigan and two dragon shifter pairs were a menace afore Lachlan hooked up with your granddaughter?"

Mary Elma pursed her lips into a thin line. "Not exactly. We understood Earth faced serious threats from multiple sources, but we didn't believe there were magical creatures involved."

"We certainly didn't," Mauvreen chimed in. She handed Mary Elma's mug back and sat next to her, rucking her skirts up around her legs. "We spent a lot of time worrying about carbon emissions and pollution and the degradation of the ozone layer."

"Translate, please," Tarika said.

Kheladin placed a foreleg under his head. "'Tis a fancy way of saying Earth is dying. While important, what's critical here is our enemies masked themselves well enough, the witches dinna know of their existence."

"The witches in question are feeling pretty damned stupid," Mary Elma snarled. "I was in the airplane the Morrigan shanghaied. The second it veered off course and ended up in magical stasis, I knew exactly what I faced. Thank the goddess, it wasn't too late to launch countermeasures."

"What airplane?" Tarika asked. "Actually, back up. What's an airplane?"

"A mechanical device that flies just like you do," Mauvreen said.

Mary Elma tightened her jaw. "The Morrigan forced the airplane off course to keep me away from Maggie. Damned Battle Crow! She knew once I got near my granddaughter, I'd be able to protect her."

Kheladin picked his next words carefully. "Magic wielders have a history of being somewhat insular because we've never trusted each other. Do you suppose if all the covens—and whoever else has magic—joined forces, we could lay our distrust aside and help one another?"

"What exactly did you have in mind?" Sharp intelligence flashed from Mary Elma's eyes as she narrowed them.

"We need to craft a plan to disable the red and black wyverns and their mages," Kheladin replied.

"What about the Battle Crow?" Mauvreen asked.

"He's hoping the Celts will step up to the plate," Mary Elma muttered. "I wouldn't be so sure of that, though." She cleared her throat. "Before you and Lachlan showed up a couple of days ago, freshly back from the fifteen hundreds, the Celts were trying to squirm out of any responsibility at all for the Morrigan."

"Aye, and their position hasna changed," Tarika pointed out. "They did the same just now in Kheladin's cave."

"What? They showed up after I left?" Mauvreen's nostrils flared.

Both dragons nodded.

Mauvreen cocked her head to one side and furled her brows. "What exactly happens if we can't corral any of them? Not the Morrigan. Not the red wyvern, nor the black, nor their respective mages."

Mary Elma opened her mouth and then closed it with a snap.

She doesna know, Kheladin thought. *Good that she's not willing to guess.*

Mary Elma fixed her dark gaze on him. "If I were to guess, dragon—yes, I've been in your mind—I fear my worst conjecture would pale against reality."

Kheladin's estimation of Mary Elma edged upward. "None of us knows, not precisely. What seems likely, since the Morrigan feeds on chaos, is she will continue to push men into battle against one another until the Earth lays in ruin, and there's nothing left."

"I suppose there's no way to kill her," Mauvreen ventured.

Tarika snorted. "She's a god. They're immortal."

"Details." Mauvreen waved a dismissive hand in the air.

"Even if we incapacitate the black and red dragons and their mages—and to do that, we'd have to sever their shifter bonds— what's to stop the Morrigan from recruiting other helpers?" Tarika asked.

"Nothing," Mary Elma snapped. "Damn it. This isn't hopeless, but it's the hardest problem I've come up against. And I've dealt with some doozies."

"If we break the bond betwixt mage and dragon, they willna be immortal," Kheladin said. "That should take care of the black and red wyverns, assuming we can catch them for long enough to sunder their bonds. The Morrigan is another problem, but we might be able to imprison her behind magical shielding."

"Who's going to provide the constant influx of magic to do that?" Mauvreen pulled a few blades of grass from the lawn and chewed on them.

"The Fire Mountain dragons," Tarika said.

"What?" Kheladin looked at her aghast. "Ye'd pollute our home?"

"If it was the only place," she said. "There's magic aplenty, and we could confine her in the depths of the mountain, where we keep dragons who've gone astray."

"How the hell would you transport her there?" Mary Elma asked.

Kheladin snorted. "Very carefully."

"I doona think so," Tarika demurred. "The Celts would have to transport her. 'Tis the only viable option."

Mauvreen spit out the grass and drank from her mug. "There's got to be a way to solve this," she muttered, "that doesn't make us beholden to them for help."

Kheladin thought the same; it was why he'd asked about the various types of mages working together for once. "I agree, mostly since they're not likely to do aught, no matter how we plead our case. Nay, we shall have to capture and hold her with brute strength."

"Not in a large battle," Tarika cautioned. "It would feed the Morrigan's battle lust and make her even stronger, and harder to defeat. As it is, she's escalating her efforts because she's frantic about Maggie and Lachlan finally finding one another."

"No shit. The prophecy is quite clear that they can weaken her chokehold on Earth." Mary Elma snapped her fingers. "I've got it. We'll split up and target each of the three separately. That way, they won't be able to bail one another out. Once the dragon shifters have been dispatched, we'll join whomever drew the short straw."

"I'm not understanding what ye mean by *short straw*." Tarika focused her whirling gaze on Mary Elma.

"Whichever one of us was unlucky enough to end up grappling with the Morrigan—alone I might add—until reinforcements show up."

"Och aye." Tarika nodded. "Mayhap that should be Kheladin or myself, or the two of us together."

"It might work." Kheladin rolled into a sit, haunches beneath him. He blew a flame-tinged gout of smoke upward. "Lachlan tapped into some verra old magic and was able to immobilize Rhukon."

"Too bad he dinna stay that way," Tarika grumbled.

"Aye, 'twas the Morrigan's doing. But if we kept her away from the other two—"

"And any other magic wielders she might seduce," Mary Elma added. "We might have a fighting chance here. I'm certain when I convene the covens, I'll get hundreds to aid us."

"What about the Druids?" Mauvreen asked.

"Maybe, but they tend to be more pacifistic," Mary Elma said.

"We willna solve this one afore Lachlan and Britta return," Tarika said. "Tell me why the air has a poison smell, and the water tastes like metal."

"Aye, and what are these weapons Maggie spoke of that could shoot us out of the sky?" Kheladin cut in.

Mauvreen and Mary Elma looked at one another. "Where to begin?" Mary Elma rolled her neck from side-to-side, making the small bones in it pop.

"We have a goodly chunk of time between now and evening when everyone else gets here." Mauvreen leaned against Kheladin's bulk. "Let's start with the Industrial Revolution, the steamships in the seventeen hundreds, and the damage they did to whales' ability to communicate over distances."

"Fine by me." Mary Elma repositioned herself to use Tarika as a backrest. "Do you mind, dragon?"

"Not at all, witch." Smoke plumed from the dragon's mouth. Kheladin sensed she was biting back laughter.

"The short version," Mary Elma began, "is men have always been greedy. They put their own gain above the good of the Earth over and over again. After two hundred years of unbridled self-indulgence, the planet's going to hell."

"Might ye elucidate a few of the steps in between?" Tarika asked. "Greed isna unique to modern times."

"Certainly." Mauvreen said. "There was a gradual shift from doing everything by hand to developing machinery that would…"

THE SUN FLIRTED with the western horizon when talk among them died down. Tarika shifted her bulk. She wove her neck around and head-butted Mary Elma gently. "Thank you for frank and thoughtful replies to all my questions."

Mary Elma got to her feet, her gaze nearly level with the dragon's. "Does this mean you've finally run out of them?"

Mauvreen joined the other witch. "The proper response," she murmured, "would be *you're welcome*."

"Sorry. Guess I need to eat something."

"We all do," Kheladin agreed.

"I smell sheep not far from here." Tarika flicked her tongue over her scaled lips.

"Not a good idea," Mauvreen said. "They probably belong to some farmer."

"They always did," Kheladin inserted, "but people used to revere us. They were proud when we picked their flocks to feed from."

"I suppose you could try the Hebrides. They're islands west of us in the North Atlantic." Mauvreen creased her forehead in thought. "Ranchers use the land for grazing but often live elsewhere."

"Might we fly there?" Tarika rolled to her feet and stretched her wings to their full extension.

"No!" both witches cried in unison.

"All right." Kheladin breathed fire and realized his temper was growing short as well. "Come, Tarika. We'll transport ourselves with magic." He turned back to the witches. "May we bring our kills back here?"

"I don't see why not," Mauvreen replied. "The wards hide you. No reason they wouldn't extend to a carcass or two."

"By the time we've returned, mayhap my bonded one will be back," Tarika said.

"You must miss her."

Mary Elma sounded warmer than she had the entire day, and once again, Kheladin revised his opinion of Maggie's grandmother.

"Aye." Tarika's voice held a wistful note. "That I do. I am worried about her as well, yet I doona wish to disturb her time with the Druid-god."

"I haven't been quite as considerate." Mary Elma grinned. "I've been checking in on Maggie and Lachlan so regularly, they finally told me to piss up a rope—at least Maggie did. Lachlan wants to stay on my good side."

"Will they be returning soon?" Mauvreen asked.

"Yes. Maggie said around six and to have something made for dinner." Mary Elma clucked disapprovingly. "I'm not sure when my granddaughter got so bossy—"

Mauvreen jabbed her in the ribs. "She comes by it honestly. Look who raised her."

"When I want your opinion, I'll ask for it." Mary Elma lifted her upper lip in an approximation of a snarl.

"You know you love me." Mauvreen draped an arm around the other witch. "Your bark's always been worse than your bite."

The corners of Mary Elma's mouth twitched into a reluctant smile. "Just don't tell anyone else, okay?"

"Doona fear." Tarika smirked. "Your secret's safe with us." She hesitated a beat. "One thing we dinna talk of is Jonathan's da. Do either of you know about his congress with the Celts?"

Mauvreen nodded, her expression solemn. "Sure do." She screwed her mouth into a disgusted moue. "The Celts are a bunch of selfish bastards, but it's a long story, and I'd rather only tell it once."

"I can wait until we're reunited." Tarika puffed smoke, and cinders drifted around her.

"Probably as good a time as any for us to be off." Kheladin moved to Tarika's side. "We shall return presently. If luck is with us, 'twill be with meat to fill our bellies."

"Do ye suppose we might scare up a cow?" Tarika asked hopefully. "There's much more meat on them than on sheep or goats."

Kheladin chuckled, blowing smoke. "Let's find out. If cattle are plentiful, mayhap we can eat a bit there and bring yet more back with us." Chanting softly, he summoned magic to transport them to one of the more remote Hebrides Islands.

CHAPTER 11

*B*ritta lay on her side, balanced on an elbow in the welter of bedclothes on Jonathan's bed. The scent of their lust lingered in the still air. She smoothed a stray dark hair off his cheek, taking care not to wake him, and glanced out the bed chamber window. The sun was moving lower in the sky. They'd have to leave soon, but she was loathe to see their few hours together come to an end. Jonathan Shea was a fascinating man, an ardent lover, and he'd just grazed the barest tip of his power, focusing on witchcraft rather than the more potent god-imbued strain that ran through him. He admitted he'd stumbled onto the deeper magic from time to time but shied away from it because it scared the crap out of him. He'd tried to discuss it with a few of the other witches, but none had been able to shed light on it, which only made him feel worse. More like a misfit. By that time, his da was long gone and no help at all.

She asked after other types of magic wielders, but beyond witches and Druids, it appeared human magecraft had died out of modern times. He stirred under her touch, breath warm on her hand. His amber eyes flickered open, and he reached for her.

"I'd love to, *mo croi*, but 'tis getting late. We should leave soon."

"You can still hug me."

"Aye, that I can so long as it doesna lead to...other things."

He grinned. "We've done those *other things* so much, I'm not sure I could get hard again, even if I wanted."

She flipped back the bedclothes and glanced at his penis. "Liar." She ran a finger over his engorged shaft. He captured her hand and pressed it against his cock. Britta settled into his arms. She fitted her body the length of his and kissed him. When he licked the seam between her lips, she drew away. "Ye're a delectable man, and I could lose myself here forever loving you, but we must join the others."

He laid a hand against her cheek, his amber gaze tender. "You miss Tarika."

"Aye. I do. Ye and she are my two loves."

"I like the sound of that." He burrowed his face into her neck and then teased the tip of her ear with his tongue.

"Wicked, wicked man. Your kisses are enough to tempt a dead woman." Shivers cascaded down her back. She pushed playfully at him, and he rose to a sitting position.

"You're probably right about leaving. We'd agreed about regrouping this evening, and it must be close to that now. Would you like a quick rinse in the shower before we dress?" He sat on the edge of the bed.

"I still canna get over how hot water flows when ye turn a lever."

He padded across the room toward the bathroom on the other side of the hall. "I'll get the water going. It won't take me but a few moments, and then the tub will be all yours."

"Ye doona wish to bathe with me?" She shot a roguish grin after his retreating form, bantering with him.

He turned slowly. "Last time we shared the tub, look what happened."

Britta got to her feet. She hoped she'd never get used to the jolt of pleasure that filled her when she looked at his sleekly muscled form. She laughed and made shooing motions with both hands. "Aye, I recall well enough. Off with you."

~

SHE WAS JUST TOWELING herself dry when fury, mingled with terror, slammed into her solar plexus.

Tarika.

Her dragon was under attack. Britta dropped the towel and sprinted for her strewn clothes, picking them up and donning them as fast as she could. "We have to leave now," she gritted out, summoning magic. "Right now."

"I thought that's what we were doing." He looked up from tying a shoe and hurtled to his feet in an instant. "What's wrong?"

"Something has Tarika."

"When? Where? Do they have Kheladin too?"

She shook her head until her red-blonde hair spilled into her eyes. "Just now. I have no idea where, nor do I know about Kheladin. I'm not linked to him."

"Put your shoes on. I'll ready a spell to get us to Mauvreen's."

"Why there? We must follow what we can of Tarika's path."

"Tarika was at Mauvreen's. The smartest thing to do would be to start there. The witches might know something. Maggie's grandmother will have been in contact with her. We need Lachlan. We need to know if Kheladin is with him or Tarika—"

Britta gave herself a mental slap. She had to get hold of herself. She wasn't thinking clearly. "Yes. Fine. Let's just go. I canna do aught from here." She shoved her feet into her shoes and bent to lace them.

When she straightened, Jonathan stood in front of her. He laid a hand on either shoulder. "We will find Tarika. I'm in this with you all the way. So's Mauvreen and the other witches."

Britta's heart twisted within her, but there was no choice in the matter. Tarika needed her, was a part of her. Even if it meant leaving Jonathan behind, she'd have to do so. "For long years, 'twas just her and me. I'm used to fighting my own battles. 'Tisn't necessary for ye to put yourself in harm's—"

He tightened his hands on her shoulders and set his jaw in a determined line. "I just told you. I'm in this with you—all the way. You're not alone anymore, Britta. You never will be again. I'm falling in love with you." The air crackled with his magic. "This isn't up for discussion. We're out of here."

~

HIS AIM WAS TRUE, but then it should've been. Mauvreen's home had been both refuge and haven throughout his life. He heard the cacophony of raised voices before the house came into view, and the walls of her familiar living room rose around them.

"Granddaughter," Mary Elma thundered. "You have to think this through. You can't just race out of here with that man."

Maggie spun to face her grandmother. Fire blazed from her blue eyes. "The hell I can't. *That man* is my husband. He needs me. So does Kheladin—"

Britta twisted out of Jonathan's embrace and stormed over to Lachlan. "Och aye, then the both of them are missing."

Jonathan hastily braided his hair to get it out of the way. It looked as if they'd be heading into some sort of fight, and he wanted it out of his eyes.

"At least our dragons are together," Lachlan ground out. "'Tis cold comfort, yet I'll grab whatever crumbs I can."

"Does anyone know what happened?" Jonathan speared Mauvreen's gaze with his and held it.

The witch shook her head. "They left here to hunt down something to eat in the Hebrides. Mary and I were just having a bite to eat ourselves when Lachlan and Maggie blew in here like a house afire."

"Hebrides." Britta narrowed her eyes. "Do ye suppose 'tis still the Selkies' home?"

Mary Elma shrugged. "I don't live on this side of the Atlantic."

"I believe so," Mauvreen said.

"Then we shall begin there." Britta exhaled sharply. "'Twas a time I knew a Selkie or two. They may have seen what happened."

"Let's go." Lachlan drew Maggie against him. The air filled with the ozone scent of his magic.

"We're all going," Mary Elma announced.

"Hold a minute," Maggie told Lachlan. She stalked to within a foot of her grandmother. "First, I'd love to have your help. I'm sure Lachlan would too. Second, you're used to calling the shots. It won't work in this group. We each have an equal voice. If you agree," she quirked both brows, "then you're welcome to join us."

"And if I'm not?" Mary Elma's voice held a silkily dangerous undertone.

"Then you and I stay here." Mauvreen shot her old friend a pointed look.

"When did you turn against me?"

"I didn't. But what Maggie said makes sense. You've never had to bow to superior magic since yours always trumped everyone else's. That's not the case here. Britta and Lachlan are much stronger than you or me."

Mary Elma pursed her lips. "If the choice is cooling my heels here and being worried sick about my blood kin, or figuring out how to fit in when I'm not the team leader, I think I can manage." A sudden, grim smile bloomed on her face. "What are we waiting for? Trails grow cold easily."

Lachlan eyed her. "Thank you. Dragon magic puts ours to shame. If something was powerful enough to spirit both dragons off this plane, we may well need far more than our combined magic to defeat it."

"Now ye mention it," Britta's voice went shrill, shy of hysteria yet not far from it, "after her initial call for aid, I havena sensed Tarika at all."

"Nor I Kheladin." Lachlan looked as if he wanted to kill something. "Which is why I think they're somewhere else in time."

Well, there's a cheery thought. Worse than hunting down a needle in a haystack.

Jonathan warded his mind. He didn't want Britta to know how rattled he was by the turn of events. He'd hoped they'd have at least a few days to explore how to blend their magic before they had to deal with Rhukon, Connor, or the Morrigan. He hadn't said anything, but who else could've made off with the dragons? Who else would even have wanted to?

"Where are we going in the Hebrides?" he asked Britta. "There are a lot of islands in that chain."

An image blasted into his mind. Britta looked at Lachlan. "Did ye get it?"

"Aye."

"You didn't ask," Mary Elma said, "but I got it too. Mauvreen?" The other witch nodded. "See you there." The air shimmered, and the two witches were gone.

Jonathan wound an arm around Britta's waist. "Shall we?" Magic crackled as he loosed a traveling spell.

"See you verra soon on the beach Britta chose." Lachlan's voice faded.

Maybe because Britta fueled his casting with her own power, a windswept, rain-washed beach formed nearly as soon as the walls of Mauvreen's home disappeared. "Is this it?" he asked.

"Aye, we did well." Britta walked toward the waves, shucking clothing as she went.

"Where are you going?"

"To visit the Selkies. 'Tis why we came to this deserted place." She turned to face him, a wild look in her golden eyes, and crooked a finger. "If you're coming, ye must follow me straightaway."

Selkies! The same manner of creature Angus had said was his mother. The wonder he'd felt at seeing a dragon resurrected itself in spades. "I'll be right behind you. Will I be able to breathe?"

"If ye doona think too hard."

For the barest moment, he wondered what she meant, and then

he slithered out of his clothing and followed her into the dark gray waters of the North Atlantic. He'd work it out somehow. Unlike many other Scottish beaches, this one dropped off quickly. He body surfed, trying to figure out where Britta had gone, when she tugged on his ankle and broke the water's surface, treading salt-smelling foam.

"Ye must either follow me or return to shore." Concern wrinkled the corners of her eyes. "There is no middle ground, nor any time for thought."

"Tell me what to do."

"Doona worry about holding your breath. Believe ye'll be able to use the water in your lungs the same way ye used air, and 'twill happen for you."

"Do you have a destination in mind?"

"Aye. The Selkies' court is a league out to sea on the ocean's floor. 'Tis easier if we swim along a diagonal course under water rather than fighting the surf."

"I'm ready."

She nodded. "If I turn and ye are not behind me, I shall find you on the beach where we left our clothes. Wait for me. I couldna stand to lose both of you."

He brushed his lips over hers, tasting the saltwater coating them both. "I'd wait until the end of time, but I'll be right behind you—at least until I drown."

Her mouth curved into a grim smile. "Ye willna drown. Draw your magic. Imagine the water is air."

Britta jackknifed her body away from him and headed for the depths. He opened his mouth to fill his lungs and then stopped. Either this would work—or it wouldn't. Instead, he linked to the rich vein of magic living within himself and dove after her. The water this close to shore was murky. He peered through it and caught a glimpse of Britta's kicking feet. He thrust himself through the water before he completely lost sight of her. Bubbles rose from his mouth and nose. With a start, he realized he was breathing. His lungs weren't seizing. He wasn't in danger of losing consciousness.

Who would have guessed?

He grinned and water rushed into his mouth. It felt natural, like it belonged there.

Britta had been right about it being easier to make headway beneath the surface swells. By the time he caught her up, they'd closed much of the distance to a structure right out of *The Little Mermaid.* Coral towers in pastel hues rose in a pattern suggestive of a castle. Glowing fish graced its corners, and some variety of numinous kelp hung from what looked like parapets.

The largest seal-creature he'd ever seen emerged from between two pylons and swam straight toward them.

"Och, aye." Britta used telepathic speech for obvious reasons. *"'Tis Aegir. I am so glad he yet lives. He was named after the Norse sea god and is just as brave."* She embraced the black Selkie, then turned and gestured for Jonathan to follow them.

He swam along behind, chiding himself for all the times he'd bypassed opportunities to learn more about other magical beings. The only thing he knew about Selkies came from children's stories. There had to be more to them than their ability to take human form, while carefully hiding their skins so they wouldn't be trapped on land. Britta had seemed pleased the Selkie sentry was still alive. How long did they live, anyway? Centuries, it appeared.

If there's ever a break in the action, I'm going to study every magical book and scroll I can get my hands on. Beyond that, if he went back to work designing computer games, he'd have way more grist for the mill.

Yeah, bet my new games could make us rich.

Then he remembered Tarika and her endless treasure. Jonathan shook his head—still tangled in wonder about almost everything— and turned his attention to the twisted coral stalks they swam around and through. Reminiscent of a maze, they reminded him of a reconstruction of the Minotaur's lair he'd visited in Knossos, except far more beautiful.

The coral opened into a grand hall. Selkies swam in small groups but formed rows once Aegir clapped his flippers together.

"Thank you for the hospitality of your welcome." Britta's words held a formal edge. *"We seek information, and there is no time to waste."*

"Introduce your associate, first." Aegir's voice was cool, guarded. *"We must know who is in our midst."*

Britta half-turned and extended a hand to Jonathan. He swam to her. Once there, he grasped her hand and inclined his head toward Aegir, saying, *"It's a pleasure to meet you."*

"I would introduce my mate," Britta said. *"Jonathan Shea is a descendant of Arianrhod."*

A murmuring susurrus ran through water far clearer than if it had been on the surface. Apparently the Selkies were familiar with Arianrhod's supposed virgin status.

"Och and ye've returned to us!" Aegir fanned his flippers at Jonathan.

He let go of Britta, flummoxed. *"What do you mean, returned? I've never been here before. At least I don't think I have."*

Aegir opened his mouth, but another coal-black Selkie with a gold circlet around his forehead eddied between him and Britta. *"Time for all that later. Aegir is king here and my son, but I still involve myself in affairs I suspect hold great import. Tell us what ye need, dragon maid. We will help if we can."*

Britta bowed low. *"My undying thanks, Sire. Tarika and another dragon came to your islands seeking sustenance. They were set upon by evil forces—"*

"Aye." The Selkie wrinkled his snout in displeasure. *"Aegir and I, along with a retinue of our knights, were near the surface. We heard the dragons trumpeting and wished to see them again. It has been long since their kind roamed the Earth."* He waved a flipper and five more Selkies swam to his side, ranging in color from pale golden to black.

Jonathan intuited these must be the knights the Selkie had referred to.

"Did ye see them disappear?" Britta leaned forward, her golden eyes a study in anguish.

Jonathan felt helpless. He wanted to protect her from anything that would cause her pain or discomfort, yet he understood he was out of his league. He listened carefully, intent on what the Selkie and his knights had to say.

"Not exactly," one of the knights, a light brown Selkie, replied.

A reddish Selkie pushed forward. *"One moment I saw Tarika—I'd know her anywhere with those bright red scales—and another dragon with copper coloring laying on their bellies in the scrub grass on the beach, gorging on fat cattle. The next a dark cloud dropped over them."*

"We couldna see through it," Aegir's father cut in, *"but it looked serious, so we rushed from the water. By the time we got to where the dragons had been, the cloud was blowing away, and the dragons were gone."*

"Och, my poor Tarika," Britta wailed. Jonathan wove an arm around her waist, trying to infuse strength into her.

"Be strong, love. We'll find her." He focused his mind voice only for her and added, *"There are many words I'd use to describe your dragon, but poor isn't one of them."*

"Tarika is resourceful," Britta murmured. *"But I still feel as if one of my arms is missing. And a chunk of my soul."*

"If there is aught we might to do to help you," Aegir said, *"ye've only to say the words."*

"Ye've already helped," Britta said. *"I know now 'twas foul sorcery that spirited them away from here. If ye might send just one knight to the beach to show us the exact spot."*

"Of course," Aegir agreed. He moved to Jonathan's side and placed a flipper on his shoulder. *"Even if ye doona remember, ye're a friend of the Selkie. Ye're welcome in our kingdom anytime."*

"Thank you." Jonathan bowed low. He was certain they could use magic to track what had happened on the beach, but if Britta felt

better with a Selkie escort, he'd defer to her judgment. After all, he was living a miracle every moment his lungs filtered oxygen from sea water. He'd never have guessed it possible without Britta's prodding.

Curiosity burned. How did the Selkies know him? Angus had apparently told the Celts his mother was a Selkie. Did that mean he'd spent time with the sea folk? Now wasn't the time to explore any of that, though. Finding Tarika and Kheladin was more important than anything else. His desire for knowledge about his origins would keep.

He swam after Britta and the reddish Selkie, who seemed to know Tarika. There was a story behind that. Jonathan was sure of it. Maybe he'd get a chance to ask the Selkie how it was he knew Britta's dragon. He wondered how much of his childhood had been spent beneath the sea. Maybe this Selkie remembered him as well—

Focus! Dragons first. Everything else will have to wait.

CHAPTER 12

As soon as Britta's head broke the ocean's surface, she saw Lachlan, Maggie, and the two witches hovering on the shoreline. Power shimmered about them like a veil. They'd apparently done enough of a reconnaissance to feel the need to protect themselves. The Selkie swam by her side. She leaned into his cool hide. "Thank you for your help."

"'Tis little enough I can do," he replied telepathically. Selkies couldn't manage human speech in their seal form.

"Och, 'tis glad I am ye remember Tarika."

Jonathan swam to Britta's other side and stroked for shore. "Is there a particular reason you remember the dragon?" he asked.

"Aye," the Selkie replied. *"When I was but a youngling, a wicked Druid found my skin and hid it from me for long years. He forced me into service, flogged me, and starved me. One day as I sat on the shore bemoaning my fate and wishing for death, Tarika appeared in the skies."*

"'Twas long afore she and I were bonded," Britta added. Shore was closing fast. She dropped her legs and felt her toes brush the rocky bottom.

"The dragon must've rescued you," Jonathan said to the Selkie.

"I have never forgotten. She found my skin almost immediately. I

130

havena laid eyes on her since that day, so when I sensed her nearby, I rushed to volunteer to be a part of Sire's retinue."

Britta walked toward the small group on shore, pulling enough magic to dry herself as she went. Jonathan joined her, and the Selkie waddled beside them, still in seal form. Britta didn't blame him for not shifting and going through the whole rigmarole of folding and hiding his skin.

Lachlan broke from the others and raced toward them. "What did ye find?" he cried.

"I brought one who saw our dragons disappear." Britta patted the Selkie's smooth hide and bent to retrieve their clothes, glad they hadn't blown away. She'd been in too big a hurry to pile rocks atop them.

Jonathan sorted his from the pile in her arms.

"Tell us." Lachlan's tone was terse. "Everything."

Britta and Jonathan dressed while she and the Selkie shared what little they knew. The Selkie showed them the place a hundred yards up the beach where the dragons had dragged their kills.

Britta examined two cattle carcasses, which were mostly bones. "At least they filled their bellies afore they were taken."

"Aye," Lachlan nodded, his face pinched with worry. "There is that."

"We traced the path of evil while we waited for you," Mary Elma, who'd been uncharacteristically silent, cut in.

"And figured out it came and went that way." Mauvreen pointed to the sky.

"I would return to the sea," the Selkie said. *"If ye have need of my race, let us know, and we will do what we can to right this misfortune."* He turned his liquid gaze on Jonathan. *"When this crisis is past, return to us. There are many who helped raise you when ye were but an infant."*

Jonathan nodded. "I'd like that."

"Thank you." Britta held out her arms. The Selkie laid his great head on her shoulder and then shuffled toward the surf. She watched his head bob in the waves until it disappeared beneath them.

She set her teeth together and turned toward Lachlan. "What think ye?"

His green eyes were narrowed in anger. A muscle twitched in his jaw. "My first guess is either Rhukon or the Morrigan, or both, spirited our dragons somewhere else in time. They must know we canna bend the strands of time without the dragons."

"What about the Celts?" Mary Elma asked.

"They werena particularly helpful a little bit ago in Kheladin's cave," Lachlan muttered.

"Probably no reason they'd have changed their minds," Jonathan agreed.

"I'm beginning to feel verra sorry I let ye talk me into the separation spell." Britta eyed Lachlan.

"How do ye imagine I'm feeling?" he countered. "It seemed a good idea at the time, with better access to each of our magics, but it doesna appear so just now."

Mauvreen sidled to Jonathan's side and hooked an arm through his. "How would you feel about asking your mother for help?"

His eyes widened as he stared at Mauvreen. "You've got to be kidding."

"No. I figure she owes you a lot since she hasn't been much of a mother."

"B-but," he sputtered. "Even if I wanted to, I wouldn't have the first idea how to find her."

"Somehow, I don't think that would be a problem." Mary Elma speared him with her dark gaze. "Mauvreen and I talked about it while we waited for you."

"Mayhap, 'tisn't such an outrageous idea after all," Lachlan said, sounding thoughtful.

"Why?" Maggie asked.

"Unless I miss my guess," Lachlan replied, a knowing smirk on his face, "Arianrhod will be in the midst of a phalanx of embarrassing questions right about now."

"Aye." Britta nodded. "I feel certain Gwydion wasted no time finding his sister and confronting her."

"Humph. So you're thinking she'd welcome any excuse to escape her fellow gods." Jonathan inhaled sharply. "Escape is one thing. Helping us quite another."

Lachlan held up an index finger. "She'll be angry and embarrassed and probably more likely to do something forbidden—like helping mortals—than if this happened afore her secret slithered out of its hidey-hole."

"I'm game." Jonathan scanned the group thoughtfully. "Any ideas how I might go about it?"

"If I'm recalling correctly, there is more than one stone circle in these islands," Britta said.

"Good call." Mary Elma clapped her hands together. "We need a place that concentrates power. One the gods can't eschew if we call them."

"Sounds like the Callanish Stones would be our best bet." Jonathan's nostrils flared. They're on Lewis Island in the Outer Hebrides." He turned to Britta. "Where exactly are we now?"

"I may not have modern names for you. But we're on the western shore of what was once called South Uist Island."

"It's the same," Mauvreen noted.

"Och, and I know Callanish well," Lachlan said. "See you at the Stones." The air shimmered around him and Maggie.

"Hold." Britta ran to him. "'Twould be safer if we formed a power circle and traveled as a group. I doona wish to lose any more of us betwixt here and there."

He clamped his jaws together. "It pains me to admit it, but ye're likely right." He flexed the arm he'd slung around Maggie.

Britta gestured to everyone. "Who's seen Callanish most recently?"

"Probably me." Jonathan stepped to her side. "I spent a holiday on Lewis Island just last year."

"We'll lend the power, ye can guide the spell."

~

THE AMOUNT of power thrumming through him was shocking. Jonathan had no idea how to command so much magic, but he felt intoxicated by the possibilities. If this was how it felt to straddle the continuum between man and god, he wanted more of it. The Callanish Stones rose around him. Their uneven obelisk shapes amplified the blend of magics, so the very air turned color—greens, blues, violet, rose—and hummed with a craving to shape spells. He'd been impressed by the Stones when he visited them, had understood why ancient magic wielders sought out power spots. In this moment, surrounded by dragon shifters and two strong witches, he recognized he'd barely tapped the beginning of the Stones' potential.

Humans strolled past, oblivious to their group. "What should we do about them?" Jonathan gestured.

"Nothing," Mary Elma said. "They won't remember a thing."

"In fact," Mauvreen flicked her fingers at two different groups, who turned toward the parking lot, "they're just leaving."

"What if others arrive?" Maggie asked.

"I'll manage them," Mauvreen said tersely. "Let's just get on with this."

"Good idea. Before Arianrhod decides to flee to another time— or world—to escape her shame," Britta added.

Jonathan placed himself between two stones and laid a hand on each. He still felt the others' magic surging through him. The stones amplified it until it crashed from side-to-side in his soul.

"Arianrhod." He called her several times. Magic built to a crescendo. He felt as if he'd laid hands on a raw power source, one that would injure him badly if he didn't stay on top of things.

"Try Mother." Britta urged in telepathic speech.

Knowing he'd have to let go of the magic soon, before it chewed him up and spit him out, Jonathan cried, "Mother," once and then again. The word felt odd on his tongue, awkward and unnatural.

"For the love of the goddess, shut up." A strikingly tall woman with silvery hair that reached the ground formed out of the mists between the stones and stared across at him out of odd-colored eyes —one gold, the other silver. She wore hunting leathers that fit her lithe form like a glove. A bow was slung over one shoulder, and knee-high leather boots laced about her lower legs.

Jonathan blinked stupidly. He hadn't expected their ploy to work. Not really. Lachlan and Britta were quick to bow. Jonathan, still feeling dazed from channeling so much magic, was slower on the uptake. He grappled for words, but his brain wouldn't cooperate.

"Well?" Arianrhod glanced from one to the other of them. "Ye summoned me. What the hell do ye want?"

Jonathan's throat tightened. He fought anger burning a path up from his belly. This might be his mother, but she didn't have the maternal instinct of a sand fly. He opened his mouth to tell her she'd been a piss-poor parent, but she stalked in front of him. Lithe as a large jungle cat, she glared at him with about as much warmth as a predator might have for cornered prey.

"Doona bother debating what to give voice to. I can read your thoughts." She brayed bitter-sounding laughter. "Even if I couldna do so, they're written plain as a scroll on your face. What would ye have me say? Your da was a very compelling man. We had a job to do together, an important one. Neither of us counted on falling in love. In a weak moment, I let my heart rule me, and 'twas my undoing." She jabbed a long-nailed finger into his chest. "I birthed you. I nursed you. Once ye dinna need me anymore, I delivered you to your da to raise. He and I made an agreement, and I kept my end."

Jonathan found his voice. "How could a two- or three-year-old child not need its mother any longer?"

She shrugged. "'Twasn't my problem. I had others to deal with. In truth, though it would've broken my heart, I expected Angus to replace me with a human woman to help with your raising."

Broken her heart? What heart?

He considered outlining the emotional poverty scarring his childhood, but it wasn't at issue here. It wasn't why they'd summoned the goddess. He cleared his throat. "Thank you for coming. We need your help."

Arianrhod narrowed her eyes. "Aye, and I thought it must be something like that."

Lachlan and Britta stepped forward. After a brief exchange of glances, Lachlan spoke for them. "Goddess. We, too, are grateful ye're here. Britta and I are dragon shifters—"

The goddess rolled her eyes and spoke over him. "I'm not stupid. I can see. I also doona sense the dragons, so I'm guessing 'tis why ye have need of me. What's happened to them? Did they get angry with you and retreat to Fire Mountain?"

Britta shook her head. "The bond doesna work that way—"

Arianrhod interrupted. "The bond I know about doesna allow ye to be separate from your dragon. Ye are in one form or the other."

"There is an older, more powerful bond…" Lachlan explained it, sketching the differences in just a few words.

"Och, so you were separate from your beasts and someone—or something—made off with them."

Jonathan nodded. "Lachlan and Britta believe they're somewhere else in time."

"Seems simple enough." The goddess spread her hands in front of her. "Why are you all still here? Why havena you begun to search?"

Lachlan blew out an impatient-sounding breath, as if he were trying to be polite. "Only dragons and Celts hold the secrets of time travel. We canna go after them on our own."

"Ah, I see." Arianrhod moved next to Jonathan and laid a hand on either side of his head. He tried to guard himself, but a shock rattled through him. The goddess looked up, a pleased expression etched on her ageless face. "My…son has the power."

He gasped, struggling to catch his breath. "M-maybe I do," he stammered, "but I'm untaught."

"Taught by witches, ye mean." Arianrhod sneered. "It comes down to much the same thing."

"I resent that." Mary Elma started toward the goddess, but Mauvreen lunged for her arm and grabbed it.

"Wise witch," Arianrhod muttered then added, "Mayhap I made a mistake by not claiming my son, yet I canna undo it now," under her breath.

"How quickly could my mate learn to bend the strands of time?" Britta asked in a clear, ringing voice.

"Your mate, eh?" Arianrhod's gaze swept appraisingly over Britta. "Can't fault him for his taste. I assume your dragon likes him too."

"Aye. Tarika adores him."

"Ye're mated to that one?" Arianrhod's eyebrows rose. "She's one of the First Born. I had a dragon lover—er…associate long ago. 'Twas a fairly close relative of hers." She cleared her throat, looking mildly chagrined by her slip. "Which other dragon is missing?"

"Kheladin," Lachlan said.

Arianrhod rolled her eyes. "I wasna thinking. Of course, your dragon would be the other one. Years back, Ceridwen tasked me with hunting for the two of you."

"Likely ye wouldna have found us." Lachlan straightened his spine. "We were ensorcelled—"

"Aye," she broke in. "By Rhukon. I'd figured out as much long ago.

Lachlan cleared his throat. "With all due respect, my lady, we need a way to track those who—"

"Do ye have any idea who or why?"

Jonathan glanced sidelong at his mother. She seemed to have no patience for allowing anyone else to finish their sentences. Lachlan answered evenly.

"Aye. We believe the Morrigan is behind this. She would maintain chaos and war on Earth until there is naught left."

"Pah! Tell me something I doona know, and she doesna work alone."

"How do you know?" Jonathan asked, curiosity burning deep. Had Arianrhod been in their minds, or did she hold new information?

"The Battle Crow has never worked alone. She co-opts others to do her bidding, discards them once she's burned them up, and finds new allies."

"In this instance, 'tis two other dragon shifters—bonded the more traditional way," Britta said. "Unfortunately, one of the dragons, Malik, was an egg-mate of Tarika's."

"Mayhap an egg-mate," Arianrhod clasped her hands before her and eyed the group, "but not one of the First Born, which means he's expendable."

"Will ye help us?" Lachlan held his hands out in a gesture of supplication.

Jonathan guessed it cost him dearly. From what he'd seen of Lachlan, the dragon shifter was a proud man. He probably hadn't asked for assistance very often over the long years of his life.

Arianrhod creased her high, patrician forehead in thought. "Ye already asked for aid from us to clip the Morrigan's wings, did ye not?" At Lachlan's nod, she went on. "We have a non-interference policy into human affairs."

"Aye." Britta stepped closer. "We know."

"We gathered to rethink our stance not so long ago, but it turned into such a bone of contention, we retreated to safer ground."

"What exactly do ye mean?" Lachlan screwed his face into a frown.

"I'll not be sharing the inner workings of the Celtic pantheon.

Let's just say we dinna find a good enough reason to alter our position."

"Oh really?" Mary Elma said, her tones thick with sarcasm. "What you mean is when the rubber met the road, you couldn't stomach censuring one of your own—let alone taking her out of the action."

"I'm not understanding about *rubber* nor *roads*, but ye will hold your tongue, witch, or live to regret it."

"You can't talk to me like that," Mary Elma sputtered, ignoring Mauvreen's frantic hand motions.

"I just did."

A corner of Arianrhod's mouth twisted into a shrewd smile and she shifted her gaze to Jonathan. "I have a suggestion. I havena been much of a mother." Jonathan opened his mouth, but she held up a hand. "Doona bother contradicting me. I see the truth of your heart in your eyes. I shall take advantage of this opportunity to train you. If we find dragons along the way, so much the better."

Smiles lit Lachlan's and Britta's faces. "Thank you," they said with one voice.

"From what that one," Arianrhod jerked her chin at Lachlan, "described, the new binding with your dragon offers you power to manipulate the time-travel tunnel as well. Ye might wish to pay close attention—to ensure ye're doing it properly."

"Could others command time-travel casting—with proper training, of course?" Mauvreen asked, sounding hopeful. "A few witches once had that skill, but it's been lost long since."

Arianrhod didn't answer right away, almost as if she were considering the question. "If what ye're asking is can ye do it with witch powers alone, the answer is likely nay. The only others I've known who can summon the time shafts—and have them show up —are those with Druid blood. And not just any Druids. They must be Druidic Seers like Jonathan."

He inclined his head toward his mother. "How shall we begin?"

The goddess scanned the group. "There are too many. I will take three, the two dragon mages and my son."

"I want to stay with Lachlan," Maggie countered. "I'm his mate."

"Your magic is green. Ye'd be nothing but an impediment."

"Mine isn't." Mary Elma straightened her spine. "Take me in her stead."

Arianrhod was silent for long moments. Finally, she shook her head. "Nay. Ye'd argue with me at every turn. I doona need turmoil. My first offer is my last. Three go with me, or I leave you to figure how to find the dragons without me."

"We accept," Lachlan said.

"What?" Fury rode beneath Maggie's words. "I love Kheladin too. I've ridden him."

"Lass." Lachlan sounded torn. "We can sort this out once Kheladin and I have returned. Ye canna bargain with the gods once they've made up their minds."

"You can't just leave me here." Maggie took a step toward him; angry color stained her cheeks. "We're stronger together. What about the prophecy—?"

Mary Elma and Mauvreen closed on Maggie, flanking her. "We shall discuss this later, child," Mary Elma growled.

"If we doona leave soon," Arianrhod said, "I may change my mind and depart without any of you." She opened her arms. Magic crackled through the air. "Get closer," she hissed. "Doona make me squander power." She skewered Jonathan with eyes that looked suddenly alien. "Pay attention…son. This may well be the only lesson ye ever get from me."

Arianrhod pursed her lips. Her gold and silver gaze shifted to Maggie. "Ye say ye rode the dragon, lass? If so, it bodes well."

Maggie's head snapped up. Hope blazed from her blue eyes. "Yes."

"Get over here. I will bring you with us after all."

CHAPTER 13

Arianrhod watched her son through hooded eyes. He'd grown into a comely man. Guilt, something she'd lived with so long, she almost didn't recognize it anymore, rose hot and acrid, and she regretted all the lost moments. Times she could've held her growing boy, shared his troubles, been a mother.

Mayhap 'twas wrong of me to do as I did.

Aye, but I had no choice. Not really.

Her thoughts turned to her magically conceived sons, Dylan and Lleu, neither of whom had comported themselves particularly well. Dylan sank into obscurity, retreating to the seas when the strain of day-to-day life without enough power to light a candle became too much to bear. Lleu would've left as well, but Gwydion subverted every single one of Lleu's escape plans as he grew to manhood. Lleu blamed her for Gwydion's meddling, and she hadn't laid eyes on him for a very long time. She suspected Gwydion hadn't, either…

Mothering wasn't part of her life path. She resented the hell out of places her choices had led, but there wasn't a damned thing she could do about it now, nor was this the time to sink into a pit of self-pity. Like she'd done hundreds of times before, she buried anything that smacked of human needs and focused on the task ahead. It helped that Jonathan was angry. If he'd been warm or, goddess forbid, forgiving, it would've torn her heart out.

Holding their traveling magic close, she prepared to summon a time shaft once she had a destination in mind. "Should we try the past first or the future?"

"If Rhukon is mixed up in this, I'd vote for the past," Lachlan said. "'Tis where he sent me when he tried to separate me from Maggie."

"Why would he have wanted to do that?" Arianrhod demanded.

"On account of the prophecy," Maggie murmured.

"Aye, ye mentioned it a little bit ago. If I knew about a *prophecy*, I wouldna have asked." Her usual irritation at lesser magic wielders prickled, but she buried it. "Answer me quickly afore I must recast our traveling spell."

"Maggie and I are Earth's primary hedge against the Morrigan's wholesale destruction," Lachlan said. "She's tried many strategies to keep us apart, so she can continue to sow chaos and poison the planet."

"With the help of Rhukon, Connor, and their dragons, she damn near succeeded." Maggie muttered.

Arianrhod pursed her lips. "Hold. Is this the prophecy where the dragon shifter and his mate—who comes to her power so late 'tis a blooming miracle she finds it at all—help drive the Battle Crow into Fire Mountain where the dragons imprison her?"

"Likely," Britta said. "We hadna heard that last, but it helps to have the endgame mapped out. Thanks."

"It also explains why they targeted our dragons." Lachlan made a rude-sounding grunt. "Without them, there's no access to Fire Mountain."

"Aye, but there is." Britta squared her shoulders. "I went alone as a maid when I had but seventeen summers—"

"The dragons would've killed you and spit you out had Tarika, or one of the others, not wished to bond with you," Lachlan said.

"Och aye, and I wasna aware." Britta sounded cowed.

Since there was little advantage in discussing Britta's stupidity as a youth, Arianrhod refocused them. "Returning to the current problem, 'tisn't likely those at Fire Mountain would welcome a prisoner they had to ride herd on until the dawn of the next age—unless a dragon escort brought her and insisted."

"Tarika actually saw the escort part as a job for the Celts," Mary Elma cut in from where she stood a few feet away. "She said as much when she offered up the Fire Mountain prison, or dungeon, or whatever they have there, to detain the Morrigan."

Hell would turn into a glacier before the Celts would drag the Morrigan anywhere, but Arianrhod didn't bother pointing that out.

"I know enough. We shall leave. We will begin our search in the past. Pay close attention to this spell, son. Come into my mind and watch its making and deployment. Both of you as well." She jerked her chin at Britta and Lachlan.

JONATHAN GRIPPED BRITTA'S HAND. Arianrhod seemed to be warming to him, but he didn't trust her. How could he? She was the same woman who'd abandoned him as a toddler. He wondered how long she'd lived. Surely the short span of his life was trivial when balanced against her thousands of years of existence.

Which means she hasn't changed at all, and I need to guard myself.

"Aye." His mother winked at him. "Ye should. Now join your mind to mine, or ye'll miss how to anchor your spell. When time traveling, 'tis essential to maintain an anchor at a known place…"

Heat rose to his face as he listened. She'd been in his thoughts, and he hadn't even tried to shield them.

"It wouldna have mattered," Britta focused her mind voice only for him. *"The gods can blow past any barriers we erect to keep them out."*

"I'll get better at this."

She squeezed his hand. *"Of course ye will. Let us learn the secrets of time travel, and then we willna need the Celts."*

A pearlescent tubular structure formed before them, and Arianrhod herded them through its maw. The walls were grayish and warm, as if the conduit were alive. Arianrhod chanted one incantation to call the working and another to seal them into it. Her magic held a pungent scent, like motor oil mixed with salt water.

"We're ready." She inhaled deeply, once, twice, and turned her attention to Jonathan. "Once ye are within the time portal, ye must take care we are the only living things inside it."

Lachlan snorted. "Kheladin and I were verra nearly trapped by Rhukon and Connor in a time portal."

Arianrhod turned her hands palms up and offered him a wry grin. "Betimes the hardest lessons are the ones we remember best."

Lachlan's face looked as if he'd bitten into something sour. He opened his mouth, but Maggie jabbed him in the ribs. Jonathan choked back a snicker. Likely, Maggie had borne the brunt of her grandmother's lectures for a long time, so she probably recognized Arianrhod's *Lecture 101* format. Aside from that, it was always better not to argue with older women. Like Mauvreen for example. He was sorry he hadn't paid better attention to some of her pontificating, though. It might've stood him in good stead.

While he was lost in thought, the bottom dropped out of his stomach.

They fell through the time tunnel. At least it felt like falling until he fine-tuned magic to stabilize himself. He wasn't certain quite how, but he still held Britta's hand. It took him a few anxious moments to realize he could control the sensation with tones. He experimented with cadence and pitch until he was confident he wouldn't crash to an unseen bottom and end up a pile of bones. Or end up a refugee lost in time somewhere.

Arianrhod made her way to him, a look of grudging admiration on her face. "Now ye have that part to hand, call on seeking magic to follow the sense of evil ye sensed on the beach the dragons were snatched from."

"How do you know where we were?"

She pursed her lips. "*Tsk.* I thought ye were smarter than that. Your mind is an open book to me. All mortals' are, but because we share blood…"

"This has a completely different feel than when Kheladin and I time-traveled," Lachlan said, sounding rattled. He and Maggie drew near.

"Of course it does." The goddess rolled her eyes with an *I can't believe you could be so stupid look* etched into her face. "Ye've been bonded to a dragon for how many hundred years and doona recognize they have their own brand of magic? Not only do they utilize these portals differently, they have their own ways of traveling that involve kinetics. That particular mechanism only moves them back and forth from Fire Mountain. 'Tis accessible to others, but only if they're marked by an old, powerful dragon."

She drew in a breath. "This trip willna be quite so rough once all of you settle a bit. Your anxiety makes things more difficult." She paused. "Were ye more used to this mode of travel, ye'd simply sit and wait it out."

"How many different time tunnels are there?" Lachlan asked. "What if ye have need of one and they're all occupied."

"It doesna work that way," Arianrhod replied. "An ancient living entity controls these time shafts. They move at will and split into whatever is needed."

"From what you just said, the time-travel tunnel is sensitive to emotion," Jonathan muttered.

"Aye, verra, but ye can figure out the fine points later. Back to sensing evil…"

"I've been trying to do just that," Lachlan said. "Tracking the feel of Rhukon, Connor, or the Morrigan. So far, I havena felt a thing."

"Might they have erased all sign of their passage?" Britta asked.

Arianrhod shook her head. "Not possible. Also unlikely they passed this way without leaving a trace of energy."

"Does that mean they didn't go into the past?" Maggie asked.

The goddess peered closely at the labyrinthine walls with their folds of flesh-like coverings. "We're only to the early sixteen hundreds. I suggest we descend at least another thousand years afore we try the other way."

Jonathan thought about it. He wasn't certain if he had any latitude at all with his mother, but he pressed forward anyway. "I can't say exactly why I think this, but I believe we should move ahead in time. Not very far, either. Maybe I've watched too many spy movies, but the best place to hide something is as close to *in plain view* as possible."

"I'm inclined to agree with him." Lachlan chanted a low note and held it. All of them slowed until they hovered in the tunnel.

"'Twill take more time if we doona find them and must retrace our steps back this way," Arianrhod argued.

"Aye, but mayhap we willna have to return to the past at all," Britta said.

The pearl-gray walls shuddered and developed pink overtones. "How long can we stay in the time portal?" Maggie asked.

A corner of Arianrhod's mouth turned down. "There isna a pat answer. We stay until it expels us. If we're not in a familiar time, we wait until it allows us entrance again."

"Fascinating that it's alive." Jonathan stared more closely at the shiny walls with their mucous-like coating.

"Och aye." Arianrhod grinned. "'Tis. Ask me later how it came to be. 'Tis far too long a tale right now. Two of you vote for the future. What think ye?" She eyed Britta.

"I agree with Jonathan. It seems if they passed this way moving deeper into olden times, I'd sense something of Tarika, yet I havena felt aught."

"Witch?" Arianrhod glanced at Maggie.

"Barely a witch as you pointed out earlier." Maggie smiled, but it was mostly teeth without any warmth behind it. "I'll do what everyone else thinks. I don't know enough to be useful here."

"Ye dinna like my comment about you coming late to your magic."

"Not much." Maggie shrugged. "But the shoe did fit. Let's get out of here if we're leaving. This place gives me the creeps."

Jonathan privately agreed with Maggie's assessment but kept his mouth shut. There was a sense of arcane magic in the time portal, with roots so deep it was unsettling. It took longer to move up the tunnel than it had to descend, almost as if something wanted them right where they were. Jonathan stole a glance at Arianrhod when he thought she wasn't looking. Her forehead was creased with worry, but she smoothed her features as soon as she became aware of his eyes on her.

"How can you tell where we are?" he asked.

"Aye," Britta cut in. "I would like to know too."

"See yon node?" Arianrhod pointed as they moved past it. "They're placed at intervals on both sides of the portal. Date ranges are carved into them, but ye need a certain magic to be able to read them. 'Tisn't as exact as ye may like, which is why we set an anchor in the time we left."

"We must've passed it," Jonathan said. "For a long time, I felt it above us, but now it's below."

Arianrhod nodded. "Our first stop is coming up. Ye said not verra far into the future. I picked fifty or sixty years."

"Pay attention." Lachlan snapped. "Use your magic. I just sensed Kheladin."

"Aye." Britta sounded so excited Jonathan's heart sped up for her. "Tarika came this way."

He breathed a sigh of relief. He hadn't been certain when he proposed the near future as a destination, yet his intuition rarely failed him. If their luck held, they'd rescue the dragons and maybe be back in modern day Scotland in time for supper.

"In your dreams." Arianrhod shot him a wry glance.

"Damn it! Stay out of my head."

"Just remember, ye called me. Not the other way round. Get ready. I will instruct the portal to disgorge us."

"Ready for what?" Maggie asked.

"Ye doona know what we will find, lass. 'Tisn't the same world ye left. There may be things trying to kill you as soon as ye emerge. Ye're scarcely immortal. Keep your wards up and be vigilant. Otherwise, there may be more of you needing rescue than the dragons."

"Will we still be in the British Isles?" Jonathan asked.

"Mayhap. Hard to say. The time tunnel has a mind of its own, which is why—"

"—we set an anchor," Jonathan finished for her and earned himself a sour look.

"Doona be cocky. Ye still doona know much, and what little ye do know can get you killed."

"Thanks, Mom."

Arianrhod rounded on him. "Doona be calling me that."

"She's right." Britta said from next to him. "Blood ties are strong. Our enemy could use the knowledge against us. They could make something from your blood to torture her or vice versa."

"Okay. Got it. Sorry." Jonathan shook his head, feeling like an idiot. "Let's move this show down the road."

"Betimes I doona understand him," Britta complained to Lachlan.

He rolled his eyes. "I have the same trouble with Maggie, but I'm getting used to her odd ways of expressing herself. Och, and 'tis time to exit. Kheladin's trail just vanished."

"Focus your power and follow me." Arianrhod's voice was stern.

The walls moved inward as if they were trying to crush them. Jonathan felt extreme compression all along his body. Even the air felt thick and sticky when he struggled to draw it into his lungs. As quickly as it had come, the pressure released. He tumbled through the air, managing to tuck his body into a ball just before he pitched onto rocky ground. "Christ!" he mumbled. "It's like being spit out of a cement mixer."

"'Tis because ye're tense." Arianrhod pushed into his mind. *"Had ye*

trusted to the one who controls the time shaft, ye'd have strolled out like I did."

Jonathan fanned magic around himself and looked for the others. Everyone had landed within fifty feet of him. He got slowly to his feet, grateful nothing was broken or sprained, and melted into the shadows of a dead tree while he scanned where they'd come out. Britta jerked her chin to one side where Lachlan, Maggie, and Arianrhod had gathered. He nodded and followed her deeper into the lifeless forest. Branches crackled beneath his boots. Jonathan drew data from his magic. It wasn't only the trees that were dead. Maybe it was just that his power didn't stretch far, but he couldn't sense anything alive—not a bird, or even an insect—as far as he could reach. A shudder oozed down his back. Surely this couldn't be Earth. Things couldn't have eroded this much in a mere fifty years.

KHELADIN STRAINED against shackles binding his wings to a brick tower. His shoulders ached. Rhukon, or mayhap his dragon, Malik, had managed to erect a barrier between him and his magic. It was there, tantalizingly close, but out of reach. Tarika was nearby. He felt her energy.

"Where are you?"

"The other side of this goddess-be-damned tower, fettered to it with iron."

Was that what blunted his power? "Is that why I canna reach my magic?"

"Aye." Tarika's single word held a bitten-off quality, as if she'd chew through her bonds—if she could reach them.

"Do ye know of any…antidote?" Tarika was old. If any dragon could get them out of this mess, it would be her.

A grim blast of laughter rocked him. "Aye, and wouldna we both like such a potion. Do ye think I'd still be here, waiting for that poor-excuse-for-a-dragon slime to return, if I had a way to free us? Mother should've crushed his egg afore he was hatched."

Kheladin felt young, naïve, stupid. "I dinna know we were so sensitive to iron. Lachlan often wears a sword, and he always carries a knife. Neither holds any effect on me."

"Usually, we aren't, but there's an exceptional amount binding us."

His next question felt even dumber, but he needed to know. "How could they have transported so much metal?"

"The Morrigan must've poured power into Rhukon since she canna work with iron, either. Pah! She's broken the covenant the Celts had with dragons to not make war on us. Och aye, and she was trying to stay in the background, but I felt her presence."

The implications sank deep. "That means they canna let us go."

"'Tis exactly what it means. The Battle Crow would have to stand for judgment afore her peers. She'd be exiled—likely to Fire Mountain."

Annoyance pushed fire up from his gullet and through his double rows of teeth. "It still feels damned unfair we'd get stuck riding herd on her."

"There's no other place that could contain her. We keep miscreant dragons imprisoned. Why not a Celt?"

He started to say because reprobate dragons had the decency to be ashamed of their foul deeds, or at least cowed because they'd been irresponsible enough to have gotten caught, but stopped himself. Mythical dragons didn't matter. What did was marshaling their forces to find a way out of their predicament. He jerked a wing again. Pain shot down his shoulder and foreleg.

"Ye willna help our cause if ye injure yourself," Tarika said.

"Do ye know where we are?"

"Aye. In the future but only a few years. Mayhap fifty or so."

Another unpleasant truth dawned. "Rhukon and the Morrigan want our mages to find us."

"Doona forget Connor. Of course they do." Another bitter laugh.

"They know they canna kill us. We're nothing but bait. The ones they really want are Lachlan and Britta. They canna kill them, but 'twill burn the heart out of them to see their mates tortured. Maggie isna immortal. I'm not so certain about Jonathan, yet both could suffer terrible punishments."

Kheladin sagged against his chains. His heart ached when he thought about Lachlan—and Maggie. Maybe this new bond hadn't been such a good idea. When they'd been forced to use one form or the other, at least they were always together. Beyond that, Tarika brought up a critical point. Maggie wasn't immortal. She'd be who their enemies would target to shatter the prophecy…

"Forgive me, youngling," Tarika said, breaking into his thoughts. "I was in your mind. I'm glad Britta isna trapped here with me, nor her new mate. This will give them opportunity to seek reinforcements and free us."

"If they're just walking into a trap, what difference will it make whether we're all here now or arrive separately?" Kheladin heard cynicism in his voice—and bitterness—but couldn't modulate either. "Besides, none of them knows how to bend the threads of time."

"Doona give up, Kheladin," she crooned. "I have been in worse places. We shall prevail. I feel it in my bones."

CHAPTER 14

"Where are we?" Maggie spoke quietly and drew a step closer to Lachlan.

Britta narrowed her eyes. "Beyond the where of it, what happened here? I canna sense a living creature nearby."

"'Tis because not so much as an insect or a bird lives in these dead trees. This is but one possible future—the one created by the Morrigan." Arianrhod jabbed her index finger at them. "If you doona care for it, you must return to your own time and make certain this doesna come to pass."

She glanced at Lachlan and Britta. "Do you sense your dragons? You can find them faster than me."

Britta closed her eyes. Jonathan felt her weave fire and air into a seeking spell. He moved to her side, ready to help, and opened his mind to hers. The roots of golden, glowing dragon magic entwined with her own power. He looked for a place to tap into both and joined her. She turned to him, a smile in her eyes. "Ye feel right in there."

"I'm glad." He took her hand in his. "It's better than you viewing me as meddling and chasing me out."

"Never." She squeezed his fingers.

"Tarika is to the west," Jonathan said once he focused his mind to follow the dragon's unique essence.

"Aye. Ye sense her too. Her magic is old and powerful, like a beacon."

He loosed magic and let it zing along the path Britta opened. An image rose of a medieval-looking tower with both dragons secured to huge irons rings in its sides.

Lachlan pounded a fist into his open hand. "Damn the Morrigan. Something stymies my magic. I see a tower, yet I canna pinpoint its precise location. The dragons are shackled with iron to blunt their power."

"Another reason the Morrigan uses human helpers." Arianrhod grimaced. "Iron dampens our power as well."

"We have to hurry," Maggie said. "The sooner we get close, the sooner we can map out a search grid—"

A faint wail reached Jonathan. "That sounded nearby. What was it?"

Britta wrenched her hand from his grip. She, Maggie, and Arianrhod raced toward the sound. He locked gazes with Lachlan. "I hope the women aren't heading into a trap," he muttered.

"They're not."

"How do you know?" Jonathan started after the women at a fast trot.

"Because my magic pings back clean." Lachlan caught him up and paced him.

"I thought there wasn't anything alive when we came out in this godforsaken spot."

Lachlan shrugged. "There is now."

They broke through the trees into a clearing. Jonathan stopped dead. Twenty people, thin as scarecrows, were dressed in rags and huddled in a tight circle. Dirt streaked their faces. Slumping shoulders screamed defeat. A witch stood off to one side, cursing under her breath. So that was why they hadn't sensed this group of people. She'd apparently shielded them with magic, but she looked so depleted, maybe her magical well ran dry. Britta stood next to her, soothing her, telling her they were from the past and meant no harm.

Maggie knelt in the dirt next to two children. One, a boy of about ten, lay still as death. For a moment, Jonathan thought he was dead, and then he picked up the faintest life energy. The girl, a little older, moaned but didn't open her eyes. "What happened to them?" Maggie asked a woman with filthy, matted blonde hair.

"What didn't?" the woman countered. "There's not enough food. The water's poison if you drink too much. It's not as bad for us, but the little ones have a harder time. It didn't help when a wild boar went after Alfie." She pointed to the boy.

So at least some animals are still alive, but they don't have enough to eat, either.

Jonathan gritted his teeth together. If they were really only fifty years into the future, he could scarcely believe how much had gone to hell in such a short time. "Where are we?" he asked the woman.

"Scotland." She bared a mouthful of yellowed teeth. "Doesn't look much like it did, eh? Nothing like forty years of war to wreck a place."

Jonathan glanced about. "Where do you live?"

"Underground. But we have to come out to hunt for food. It was what we were about when the boar attacked us, and then Deirdre," she pointed to the witch, "said we must be still because others were nearby."

"We won't hurt you." Jonathan's heart ached for the scraps of humanity in the clearing. He clamped his jaw tight to keep from screaming his horror and disbelief to the skies and vowed he'd do damn near anything to make sure this particular future never happened.

"I'm a doctor." Maggie ran her hands over the children's limp bodies.

The girl, who looked about twelve, moaned again, and Jonathan recognized it as the same sound that caught their attention in the first place.

"So?" A dark-haired man with a deeply seamed face stepped forward. "I don't see your bag or any medicines."

"She's a witch, that one," the resident witch, still standing next to Britta, said. "Maybe she can do more than you think."

Maggie worried her bottom lip between her teeth. She rotated her body so she looked at Lachlan. "Go. Get the dragons. Come back for me once you're done. I'm afraid if you wait—"

"Are ye sure?" Lachlan strode to her side and bent to kiss the top of her head.

Maggie nodded. "My magic's good for healing. I'd just be in the way where you're going."

"Good call." Arianrhod nodded approvingly. "I knew there was a reason I changed my mind and allowed you to come. We should be off. We may still have the element of surprise."

"Tarika knows I am here," Britta said.

"Aye, Lachlan's dragon likely does, too, but would they be so stupid as to alert their captors?" Arianrhod shot back.

Britta bristled. Jonathan loped to her side and put an arm through hers. *She didn't mean anything by it.*

"I heard that." Arianrhod laughed. "Nay, those like me were born abrasive." She gestured toward Maggie. "Pay attention, witch. If I call for you, ye must drop whatever ye are about and come immediately."

"I understand." Maggie held the boy in her arms and began a low chant over him. The small body relaxed against her. "He's the worst. If I can save him, surely I can mend the girl too." Magic rose around her, rich with the soothing scent of lilacs, and the cadence of her chant soared.

"Cast your invisibility spell again, witch," Lachlan instructed the woman standing outside the small group. "See my mate remains safe." At her nod, he moved to Arianrhod's side.

Deidre nodded. Black hair, chopped off at shoulder length,

bobbed around her weary-looking face. For the barest moment, Jonathan detected a gleam of hope in her green eyes.

He walked toward Arianrhod with Britta by his side, and the spell to transport them enclosed him immediately. "We don't want to come out on top of them," he cautioned.

"'Tisn't likely since we doona know exactly where they are. What is it with all of you? I scarcely require instructions." Arianrhod muttered angrily in Gaelic as Lachlan joined them.

"Ready when ye are," Lachlan said a shade too brightly. Maybe he was trying to smooth things over.

Jonathan glanced sidelong at his mother. She might not need instructions, but a crash course in manners was long overdue. *Abrasive* didn't come close to describing her high-handedness. He shuttered his mind. No matter how he felt about her, he could learn from her, and he'd be wise to take advantage of the opportunity.

BRITTA KEPT BREATHING. Being afraid for Tarika was a new experience. The dragon had always been the stronger of the two of them, and Britta had difficulty understanding how she'd allowed herself to be captured. Arianrhod's spell spit them out on a bleak, barren-looking plain, a very different British Isles than the place she knew. The green, verdant aspect was gone. Had it stopped raining? The woman in the clearing said the water was toxic, so it must've worsened substantially from Jonathan's time.

"Look what that bitch of a crow has done to our lands," Arianrhod exclaimed, shaking her head angrily.

"She'd like it this way," Lachlan said. "The less likely a place is to support life, the better it feeds into her plans to turn Earth into one big battlefield, where she can stalk from one corpse to the next, tasting their blood."

"If she kills off everyone, there willna be any more battles to feed her bloodlust," Arianrhod snapped.

"We should make a point of telling her. Fucking bitch." Jonathan spat on the ground.

Arianrhod laughed grimly. "Sure, and that will make all the difference."

Jonathan tapped the side of his face where she'd slashed him with her beak. "This might be mostly healed, but it still burns as if she poisoned me.

"Och," Lachlan muttered. "Like as not she did. I'm sick to death of this. First Kheladin and I were swept into a sleeping spell. Once we wakened, 'tis been a constant attack on us—or Maggie."

"And now Tarika and I," Britta cut in. "We must take this in stages. Once the dragons are free, we can figure out what to do with Rhukon, Connor, and the Morrigan."

"Ye doona give orders here." Arianrhod's gold and silver gaze pierced Britta. "The reason I dinna bring the crone-witch along was she would've challenged me at every turn."

"Fine." Britta bit off the word. "Battles united under a single commander have greater chance of success. What comes next...goddess?"

A winged shape took form on the horizon, flying toward them.

"We're about to find out." Arianrhod planted herself, feet apart, hands on her hips.

The Morrigan fluttered to the ground a few feet away and shimmered into one of her human forms. She looked like a hag, with stringy black hair, sunken black eyes, and a shapeless body swathed in black robes. "'Tis ye!" A surprised look washed over her face.

"Aye, one of your fellow gods." Arianrhod sneered. "Ye have broken the covenant betwixt us and the dragons. I am come to bring you to justice."

A crafty look stole into the Morrigan's eyes. "The other Celts will let me go."

"We doona know that," Arianrhod countered. "I canna remember the last time a Celt imprisoned a dragon. It may never have happened afore."

"I'll free them." The Morrigan tried for a bright smile. She rubbed her hands together. "We can pretend this never happened."

Lachlan grunted something, but Arianrhod held up a hand. "Free the dragons, and we shall talk further."

The Morrigan narrowed her eyes as if she sensed a trap. "Ye must give me your word, Celt, afore I loose them."

"Really?" Arianrhod cocked her head to one side. "Ye'd ask me to break the covenant right along with you?"

"Um, aye. Equal guilt and all." The Morrigan grinned, displaying badly stained snaggle teeth.

Arianrhod blew out a breath and tilted her chin up. "I doona know when ye decided ye could play sovereign over the rest of us." Power crackled from her outraised hands. The Morrigan's robe began to smoke, and she batted at it. "The way I see it," Arianrhod continued, "your only chance at clemency is to cooperate. Ye've already been caught."

The Morrigan shifted her gaze downward and studied the parched earth intently. Britta could almost feel her mind working. She chafed at just standing, talking, though she recognized Arianrhod's wisdom. It might take hours to unravel whatever magic held the dragons, particularly since iron was involved. Time passed. Finally, the Morrigan gave a terse nod.

"I have just instructed my...comrades to unshackle the dragons."

"Nay!" Lachlan strode forward. "Britta and I will do that. Drop whatever magic ye're shielding the precise location of that tower with, so we doona waste as much as a minute hunting for it."

Tarika burst into Britta's mind. *"Hurry, bondmate."*

Jonathan must've heard because his expression softened. He caught her eye, nodding encouragement.

Lachlan raised his arms skyward in anticipation. "Kheladin may be young and untried, but I love him. He's a part of me."

"See what mischief ye've wrought," Arianrhod spat at the

Morrigan.

"Aye." The crone's smile broadened. "Misery. Wretchedness. Desolation. Gloom. I love them all. They feed me."

Britta rounded on her. "What an unnatural creature ye are. Even Arawn, god of the dead, holds respect for living creatures. Dragons are beasts out of legend. How could you—?"

Lachlan beckoned to her, his expression grim. "I found them. The Morrigan must've complied with my request."

"Go," Arianrhod cried. "We shall join you presently, once I've figured out what to do with her." She jerked her thumb at the Morrigan.

Britta leapt to Lachlan's side. He summoned power to transport them. Seconds later, an enormous, crumbling stone tower came into view. She heard someone shrieking, realized it was her, and raced forward, intent on Tarika, straining against thick chains.

"By the goddess," Britta swore, revolted by the sight of her dragon suffering. "How could anyone have done this to you?"

"Take care!" Lachlan shouted as he hurled toward Kheladin. "We doona know for certain that the Morrigan hasna left us a few unpleasant surprises."

"Stop!" Kheladin's voice rasped as if he were in pain. "A barricade stands betwixt you and the chains."

Britta screeched to a halt, digging her heels into the hard earth. She sent power skittering outward and found a huge barrier circling the tower. Beginning at ground level, it was at least twelve feet high, constructed of multiple bands of intertwining magical ropes thicker than the chains binding the dragons. She stared at it, thinking, and then walked closer. The nearer she got, the weaker her magic became. Britta slapped her forehead with a palm, turned, and put some distance between herself and the fell magic circling the tower. When she could think clearly, an idea slammed into her.

Of course. I'm making this too hard.

"Lachlan! If we work together, we can defeat it."

"What do ye mean?" He cast a plaintive glance at Kheladin before loping to her side. "Soon," he told his dragon.

Britta held up a hand. "Tarika. If we blast through the chains, can ye fly through the barrier?"

"Aye. It never was a problem. The Morrigan constructed it sloppily, mayhap because she assumed we'd never escape iron chains."

"Your idea," Lachlan demanded in a sharp voice. "Och aye. Sorry, I dinna mean to be rude."

"Can ye gin up enough power to cut through their chains?"

"Of course."

She nodded sharply, and a feral grin split her face. "The barricade may not be elegantly constructed, but it's enormous, and it dampens my magic if I get too close. I will create an opening, but I will do it from here. 'Twill be far simpler, and much faster, than dismantling the entire thing—"

"Brilliant!" Lachlan clapped her on the back. "Do it. I'll funnel my magic through the opening and free the dragons."

Britta focused her attention—and her power. It was harder than she imagined and took three tries before the hole was big enough Lachlan's magic wouldn't boomerang back and hurt them.

"Aye!" she shrieked as a steady stream of power poured from Lachlan. "'Tis working." Iron creaked and clattered; chains shattered and fell to the ground, raising choking clouds of dust. "Thank the goddess—"

Wingbeats drowned out her words. Tarika descended in a flurry of leathery wings and scales. The dragon lifted Britta in her forelegs and hugged her tight. When she looked up, Lachlan was astride Kheladin, arms as far around the dragon's neck as he could manage. The muscles in his face and neck rippled, and he looked as if he were holding onto his male dignity by the thinnest of margins.

Britta's cheeks were wet, and she realized she was crying. Gemstones clinked around her. Dragon's tears. "Aye, dragon shifter," Tarika said. "My dragon shifter. 'Tis glad I am to be reunited."

"Where's our mate?" Kheladin asked Lachlan.

"Caring for sick children. We'll go to her as soon as we're done here."

"We are done. Time to return to the others," Britta said. "The sooner we finish what we've begun, the better."

"Fine by me," Lachlan called from Kheladin's back. He and the dragon took to the skies.

After a final hug, Tarika settled Britta onto her back. She spread her leathery, red wings and followed Kheladin and Lachlan. They touched down near where Arianrhod and the Morrigan faced off against one another. Jonathan stood near his mother. The moment he saw her and Tarika, he sprinted toward them.

He wound his arms around the dragon's body and she bathed him with steam, murmuring in Gaelic. "I'm so glad to see you," he repeated. "Thank fucking Christ you're okay."

"'Tis impossible to kill me," Tarika breathed still more steam, "but your kind thoughts are appreciated."

Britta watched Arianrhod sidelong, and felt new respect growing. The goddess was both ancient and wise, even though Jonathan's father may have caught her at a weak moment. And mayhap a few other men as well. She jumped lightly down from Tarika and hugged Jonathan, before walking to the goddess's side. "What do ye need from us?"

Arianrhod looked down her nose at the Morrigan. "About those comrades of yours…"

"I suppose they're long gone." Lachlan sneered. "Neither Rhukon nor Connor were ever known for their courage."

"Neither were their dragons." Kheladin blew a huge gout of fire. It landed scant inches from the Morrigan's battered boot toes. He stalked close enough to the Morrigan to touch her, but she stood her ground and eyed him balefully. "Bring them here," Kheladin demanded.

"Who?" The Morrigan tossed her head.

"The dragons—or their mages," Lachlan clarified. "Bully idea, Kheladin." Still astride the dragon, he slapped its neck.

"Why, thank you." The dragon mock bowed.

"An excellent idea." Tarika trumpeted. "I like it." She turned her whirling eyes on the Morrigan and added slyly, "'Twould make you look better when Arianrhod drags you afore the other Celts."

"It might at that." The Morrigan squared her shoulders and morphed first into a lissome maid and then into three women. Tall, beautiful, and terrible, they stared at the group out of flat, dead eyes. Long, blonde hair eddied about shimmery blue robes.

"We would leave," they said in unison.

"I bind you," Arianrhod chanted. "You may leave, but to me you must return. Now and always until I release you."

"We understand." The air around the trio twinkled. In moments they were gone.

The Morrigan in all her forms...

Fear rocked Britta to her bones. One of the oldest tales predicted when the Morrigan split into Badb, Macha, and Anann, destruction would follow in their wake. "'Tisn't a good omen. Can aught be done?"

Arianrhod turned to her. Something akin to compassion glinted from the depths of her multihued eyes. "Och aye. Look about you, lass." She spread her arms wide. "The best gift we could give mankind, and the Earth, would be to make certain *this* future never becomes primary."

"I remember what was predicted when the Morrigan split," Jonathan said slowly. "It wasn't good."

"Nay," Lachlan concurred. "It certainly wasn't. Kheladin, when Rhukon and Connor show up, what do ye have in mind."

The copper dragon wound his neck around so he looked at Lachlan. "First, we immobilize them, and then we haul them to Fire Mountain."

"It could work." Tarika wrinkled her scaled brow. "But only if we separate dragons from mages and kill the mages."

"Easy enough. They willna be immortal once the bond is broken," Britta said.

Kheladin blew flames skyward. "Aye, 'twill certainly help with the killing part."

Jonathan shook his head. "Help me understand. When Britta and Tarika separated, they did so willingly. Can you force a dragon and his mage apart?"

"I can do that. So can the Morrigan," Arianrhod said, a grim smile in place. "Convenient she's on no one's side but her own."

"Aye, and right now she's motivated to save her own hide," Britta cut in.

"That was a refreshing bit of strategy you used with her." Jonathan walked to Tarika's side and stroked her red scales. "I didn't think she'd fall for it."

Arianrhod snorted and crossed her arms over her chest. "I'm ashamed I dinna think of it first. I caught her dead to rights. You notice she dinna bother denying she'd broken the covenant. We canna lie. 'Tisn't in our makeup."

"So when Tarika suggested tossing Rhukon and Connor under the bus," Jonathan said thoughtfully, "the Morrigan jumped on it with both feet."

"*Under the bus?*" Britta asked.

"Aye, what's a bus?" Lachlan looked confused.

"It's just an expression," Jonathan clarified. "Sort of like forcing someone out onto a tree branch and sawing it off."

"I understand. Ye box someone into where they have no other choices." Britta beamed at him and then turned to Tarika. "Malik was your egg-mate…" She let her words trail off.

"Doona fear." Tarika puffed fire and smoke. "It willna soften my heart toward him. He's been naught but trouble since he hatched."

"They're returning," Arianrhod cautioned.

"Mount behind me," Britta shouted to Jonathan and vaulted onto her dragon. "Once the fighting begins, we'll strike from Tarika's back."

CHAPTER 15

Jonathan straddled Tarika. He settled Britta firmly against his body and wrapped his arms around her. God, she felt good against him. And to be astride the dragon was little shy of amazing. Heat sifted into him through her scaled hide.

"Doona drop your guard." Britta focused her mind voice only for him, her body vibrating with tension. *"We're far from out of danger."*

"What are ye doing?" Fury made Rhukon's voice shrill. His form first wavered, then faded and solidified, about twenty feet away.

"Aye," Connor squealed once he came into view. "We're on your side. Remember?" He broke and tried to run, but Arianrhod flicked her fingers at him, and he sprawled on his ass. He still lay on his butt in the dirt when Badb, Macha, and Anann took form. The sisters stood behind the men. Jonathan saw the spell the trio wove, boxing them in from every side.

"On your feet." Badb, Macha, and Anann spoke in unison.

Jonathan wondered if they ever did anything but. Connor rose in a jerky, puppet-like fashion, as if he were attached to marionette strings. The three women herded him next to Rhukon.

Jonathan eyed the two dragon shifters. Both men were ashen. Sweat beaded Rhukon's pasty skin. Even his dark hair looked defeated. Connor's dandified good looks, with his red-gold curls and sky blue eyes, were out of place in the austere landscape stretching around them. Both men wore formfitting battle leathers. Maybe they'd planned to return to the Middle Ages once they did the Morrigan's bidding. Up close like this, they didn't look like much of a threat, certainly not one potent enough have wreaked as much havoc as they had.

Rhukon straightened and shifted his gaze from one of the Morrigan's forms to the others. "I asked what ye're doing. We've served you well—"

"Enough." One of the sisters spat out the word.

That answers one of my questions. They can speak independently.

"Ye were a fool to trust the Morrigan." Tarika took a few steps closer, addressing her words to Rhukon. "She's on no one's side but hers. Even among the Celts, she's never been known for collaboration. I would speak with your dragons. There is deep shame in their role in this."

Arianrhod drew closer to the three sisters but aimed her words at Tarika. "I will help. What ye've wrought offends me."

"We thank you." The trio was back to speaking as a unit, but they didn't respond to Arianrhod's criticism.

Lachlan and Kheladin moved closer. "Ye may have noticed Britta and I are separate from our dragons," Lachlan said.

Rhukon sneered. "Aye, I've been trying to puzzle out why ye broke the bond. Did your dragon tire of you?"

"Och, ye're such an ass," Britta gritted from between clenched jaws. "Malik should be ashamed he bonded with you. I'm ashamed for him."

Rhukon rolled his eyes.

"We waste time." Arianrhod dropped a hand onto Rhukon's shoulder and began to chant.

He squirmed to escape her grip, and then he batted at the

goddess, trying to grab or punch her, but she controlled him easily. One of the trio did the same to Connor.

"They'll force the bond into the open and then break it," Britta said, not bothering with telepathic speech.

A panicked expression widened Rhukon's eyes until white showed all around his pupils. Clearly intuiting what was coming, he intensified his efforts to escape from Arianrhod. Malik formed in the air above him, black scales gleaming in weak sunlight. Preki, red scales ablaze as if lit from within, took shape behind Connor.

"Thank Dewi!" Preki invoked the Celtic dragon goddess. "I've wished to be free from this hapless human forever."

"My feelings exactly." Malik snorted fire. He bowed toward the Celts, head graceful on his sinuous stalk of a neck. "Thank you for freeing us. Thanks to you as well, sister and egg-mate." He nodded toward Tarika.

"Nice try." Tarika scoffed. "As one of the First Born, I command you to stay where you are while we deal with the humans you were ill-advised enough to join your lives with."

"We hear and obey." Preki bowed his head in a twin gesture to Malik's.

"They're very beautiful," Jonathan said near Britta's ear.

"Doona let them fool you. Unlike the Celts, dragons lie all the time. They're far from stupid, and they doona wish to spend their life in a cage deep within Fire Mountain."

Malik focused his whirling dark eyes and hissed at Britta.

"Ye willna do that again to my bondmate." Tarika didn't raise her voice, but command rang in it. Malik hooded his eyes.

"How would ye die, mage?" Arianrhod shook Rhukon as if he weighed nothing.

"I would rather not, my lady."

"Too late. I give you two choices. Ye may try to redeem some pride and die in open combat against Lachlan or Britta—or me."

Rhukon swallowed hard. Jonathan saw his throat working. "My second choice?" he croaked.

"I snap your neck where ye stand."

Rhukon sucked in a breath, and then another. He spread his hands in front of him. "Surely ye'll reconsider. One such as myself, a powerful mage with magic honed by centuries of practice—" His hands flew to his throat. He grappled with it, gasping for air. His skin developed a definite bluish tint. Arianrhod released him and shot an annoyed glance at the three sisters.

"I tired of his whining," one of them said and voiced a guttural curse.

Blood spewed from Rhukon's nose and mouth, spattering Arianrhod. He crumpled to the ground, making gurgling noises as he choked to death on his own fluids.

"Ye may have tired of him at this late date." Arianrhod grimaced and wiped gore off her face. "But he was my prisoner. Like as not, ye dinna wish me to hear what he might say against you."

All three sisters turned eerie, matching grins on Arianrhod. "The end result is all that counts," they said as a unit. "Dead is dead, and ye're correct. The dead carry no tales."

Their grins widened until Jonathan had to look away from their ghoulish expressions, his stomach twisting in disgust.

Connor jerked away from the sister holding him. He threw wards around himself and raced across the hard-packed earthen plain.

"He's mine." Britta's voice rang out. With powerful wingbeats helping to propel them forward, Tarika brought them abreast of Connor's fleeing figure and settled in front of him, blocking his path. Britta raised both hands. Power blazed from them, catching Connor midstride. Tarika added dragon fire to the mix, and the mage turned into a pillar of flame, screaming in agony.

The smell of burnt flesh was cloying. It stung Jonathan's nose and throat, but he was glad the bastard was dead. It shocked him. He'd never hated anyone enough before to want them dead. The desperate state of the future changed all that. He'd still be alive fifty years from now, and he didn't want to live in a place like this, a place stripped of life.

Bloodlust poured from Britta and her dragon in crimson waves. It felt right. For the first time, he pictured himself a warrior and felt confident he could hold his own if the shit hit the fan, and he had to defend home, hearth, family, and country.

Tarika half-hopped, half-flew, to Malik and Preki. "Kheladin," she called. "I would have your assistance."

"First Born." Malik inclined his head. "Thank you for—"

"Be quiet, traitor, or I'll have your tongue," Tarika snarled. Malik's jaws snapped shut. Preki's nostrils flared. Smoke poured from them. Kheladin strode to Tarika's side with Lachlan astride him.

Arianrhod stood off to one side, a satisfied smile on her timeless face. Jonathan tapped into her mind, tentative at first, but she sucked him in and said, *"Nothing quite so satisfying as seeing your enemies fall—no matter who kills them. Never forget that...son."*

"I'm glad they're dead. Look what they've done to the Earth." Loathing filled him. Rather than burying it as he would once have done, he embraced it.

"It wasna so much them as the Morrigan." Arianrhod moved her gold and silver gaze to the three sisters, who looked like carved statues. "Your triple form is no longer needed."

Power blasted across the clearing. When it cleared, the crone was back with a smirk on her lined face. "Shall I dispatch the dragons next?"

"Nay!" Fire streamed from Tarika's jaws. "Dragon justice isna yours to command."

"I could help," the Morrigan insisted sweetly.

"The best help from you would be to mend the damage ye've done to Earth," Arianrhod snapped.

The Morrigan shrugged. For a moment, she took her crow form and then flickered back to human. "Sorry. I destroy. Creation isna within my powers."

Arianrhod huffed. "Mayhap ye could work on developing some new skills."

Tarika nudged Kheladin. "Will ye accompany me to make certain these two return to Fire Mountain?"

The copper dragon inclined his head. "'Twould be an honor."

Malik shook his head until his shiny black scales clanked against one another. "What if I doona wish to go?"

"Ye have no choice…egg-mate," Tarika hissed.

"Aye." Kheladin trumpeted. "Look at the destruction ye've shaped. Ye canna be trusted to run free."

"Ye gave our mages a choice." Preki spoke for the first time. Compulsion ran beneath musical words.

Tarika bared double rows of teeth. "Would ye rather a fight?" At the red dragon's nod, she spat into the dirt. "Ye realize Kheladin and I are immortal. Ye are not."

"I would prefer an honorable death than millennia shut up in the bowels of Fire Mountain."

"Humph." Malik snorted fire. "Speak for yourself."

Tarika sucked in a noisy breath. "'Twill be one way or the other. The same for both of you. Fire Mountain or combat."

"Ye always were nothing but a troublemaker." Malik spun, using his tail for a balance point, and blasted Preki with fire.

Obviously taken by surprise, the red dragon yelped as fire raked his scales. Jonathan figured fire couldn't hurt the dragon. He was probably more shocked his companion had turned on him than anything else.

"What do ye want to do?" Britta asked Tarika.

"We shall see how this plays out." The red dragon crossed her forelegs across her chest. "Mayhap 'twill be one less to worry about."

Kheladin nudged them. "Isna there some way to, er, resocialize them? There are so few of us. I hate to lose any."

"Aye. It hurts my heart too, yet these dragons hatched weak or they'd not have been seduced by darkness." Tarika curved her neck toward Kheladin and laid her cheek against his. "Ye're kind-hearted and compassionate. Excellent traits. Doona lose them."

The din of battle grew louder. Malik and Preki stood about fifty feet away from one another trading jolts of magic interspersed with fire. The air thickened with smoke, the smell of ozone, and dragon cries. Blood streamed down Malik's chest. Jonathan hunted for a wound and found it on the side of the dragon's neck.

The black dragon spread his wings. "He's trying to leave," Jonathan shouted.

"He willna get far," Kheladin said.

"Aye, if Preki doesna shoot him out of the skies, I will." Tarika nodded grimly.

Malik rose into the air. Preki spread his wings but apparently changed his mind. Jonathan could almost see the red dragon's thought processes. He focused his magic and heaved a great burst at Malik's unprotected underside, splitting him from crotch to breastbone. Malik screamed. His great black wings beat the air once, twice, and then he plummeted to Earth.

The black dragon hit hard, with a thud that rocked the ground beneath them. Sparks rose around him.

Tarika began to chant. Kheladin joined her. At intervals, Britta and Lachlan chimed in. Malik's form shimmered in the still, dead air of Earth's future. It developed an iridescent quality just before it vanished.

"What did you do?" Jonathan asked Britta.

"Sent his soul to its rest in Fire Mountain."

"Aye, and scattered his remains through the ages so no one might stumble upon his carcass and siphon residual power from his bones," Tarika said. She turned to Preki. "Ye comported yourself admirably."

The red dragon bowed. "Thank you, First Born."

"Do ye have a choice of who ye would face next?"

Preki sneered. "Ye mean, who do I chose to kill me?"

"However ye wish to phrase it." Tarika inclined her head.

"Of course, I pick Kheladin." Preki raised his snout. "He is young, untried."

Kheladin breathed fire. "Ye think so?"

"Do ye wish me astride you?" Lachlan asked.

"Nay. I will do this on my own."

The copper dragon drew himself up proudly. Lachlan jumped to the ground. Britta and Jonathan joined him. Kheladin's green eyes whirled in what looked like anticipation. Jonathan recognized savagery. The dragon was immersed in it. Kheladin wanted Preki's head on a stake.

"Ground or air?" he snarled.

"Open choice," Preki snarled back. "Too hard for you?"

"Open choice 'tis. We can pick wherever we fight best."

Fire blasted from Kheladin's mouth and was met with an even bigger gout from Preki. Smoke filled the air. Jonathan's lungs burned if he inhaled too deeply. Britta leaned toward the battle and skinned her lips back from her teeth. Lachlan moved to her other side. "Doona help him," he said softly.

"Just a little bit?" Britta turned her golden gaze on Lachlan.

"Nay. He must do this on his own. Kheladin is wise and strong. Believe in him. I do."

"It goes against the grain to kill one of their own," Britta murmured, and Jonathan understood she'd do whatever was needed to make certain Preki's soul joined Malik's. He loved her fierceness, and her absolute devotion to dragonkind.

A dragon screamed. Jonathan's head snapped up. Kheladin spit blood from a gash down one side of his face. Jolts of power—more than seemed possible—flew at him.

Shit!

"The Morrigan," Jonathan shrieked at Arianrhod. "She's helping Preki."

The goddess hurtled to the Crow's side, slapping wards around her. "What in Danu's name do ye think ye're doing?" Arianrhod screeched.

The Morrigan shrugged. "'Tis the thrill of battle. Sometimes I forget myself. No harm done. Both dragons yet live."

Yes, but if I wouldn't have noticed what she was doing and called her off...

In that moment, Jonathan recognized it would take years, maybe the entire rest of his lifetime, before he understood the Celtic gods. They lived by a code so different—brutal, bloody, feral—he could only imagine its origins. Britta had been ready to add her magic to the bloodletting too, but he accepted her savagery. He shook his head. He had lots of sorting out to do, and here wasn't the place.

Lachlan moved closer to the fighting. Kheladin trumpeted. He twisted and dove to evade Preki's magic. Where the dragons' power collided, sparks filled the air and great, booming noises made Jonathan's ears ache. Preki screeched a protest and grappled with a foreleg where it hung useless against his chest. Kheladin feinted from side-to-side. In a sudden, bold move, he launched himself at Preki and closed his jaws around the other dragon's neck. Blood geysered, showering everyone with viscous red-gold drops. The sharp, metallic scent filled Jonathan's nostrils.

It smelled like victory.

Maybe I've discovered my own feral underpinnings.

The thought was electrifying in an odd sort of way.

Preki lashed his trapped body furiously, but Kheladin held fast, even when the other dragon maneuvered them into a boulder pile and bashed Kheladin against a huge rock. It took all Jonathan's self-control not to pull magic to help Kheladin. When he glanced at Lachlan, the mage's jaw was tight, and he'd balled his hands into fists. Lachlan loved his dragon. Loved him enough to let him fight his own battle.

"This must be damn near killing him," Jonathan said to Britta and tilted his head toward Lachlan.

"Aye," Britta said, "but 'tis nearly over."

Almost as if her words were prophetic, Preki's thrashing slowed and then weakened. Kheladin didn't let go until his adversary stopped moving. The dragon opened his mouth and dropped the red dragon in the dirt, panting. Preki opened one eye, but it was already glazing over.

"Send him to his rest without me." Kheladin turned away. Lachlan sprinted to his side, but the dragon shook him off. "I would be alone for a short time, bonded one, to make peace with what I have done."

"As ye will. Ye were strong and brave. Ye have my utmost respect." Lachlan bowed to his dragon.

The moment was so poignant, it thickened Jonathan's throat, and his eyes sheened with unshed tears.

Britta, Tarika, and Lachlan chanted over Preki's corpse until the dragon disappeared. The group held a respectful silence waiting for Kheladin to rejoin them.

"Thank you." Kheladin inclined his head. "I couldna both kill him and wish peace for his soul. I hated him while I fought him, and I hate him still."

"We understand." Tarika touched snouts with him.

Jonathan turned to Arianrhod and the Morrigan. "What happens next?"

Arianrhod squared her shoulders. "I'll escort this one," she jabbed the Morrigan in the side, "back to our people. She has much to answer for."

"I go willingly." The Morrigan smiled. It cut across her face like a scimitar might have. "Let all who are here note my willingness."

"Kheladin and I will retrieve Maggie, and then we shall return to our own time," Lachlan said.

"Och aye. We shall join you." Britta took Jonathan's hand and squeezed hard.

"In case we lose one another en route," Lachlan eyed the group, "mayhap we could gather at Mauvreen's."

"Done." Tarika slapped her tail on the ground. "There's room for Kheladin and me there, without having to fold ourselves within our bondmates' bodies."

"Hurry." Kheladin looked pointedly at the place on his back where Lachlan rode. "I miss Maggie."

Lachlan grinned. "Now ye mention it, so do I." He vaulted to the dragon's back and the dragon spread his wings, taking to the pollution-rimed sky.

"There's much to discuss," Britta said quietly. "I see questions behind your eyes."

Jonathan nodded and moved to face his mother. "Will I see you again?"

She quirked a curious brow. "Would ye like to?"

He thought about it. "Maybe. I'm not sure." He answered as honestly as he could. "Could you tell me about Da and what your kin wanted with him?"

"Aye. That I could. Or—"

"If she willna tell you, laddie, I'd be glad to oblige." The Morrigan leered at him from her rheumy, crone's eyes before shifting her focus to Arianrhod. "Son of a bitch. He's your son. Fascinating. *Virgin huntress.*" Spittle flew from her lips as she dissolved into cackles.

"Quiet!" Arianrhod thundered, but the Morrigan didn't even slow down.

"Sorry." Jonathan turned away.

Arianrhod snaked out a hand and gripped his upper arm. "Doona be. I grew weary of the deception after all these years." She pulled on his arm until he had to turn to face her. "Let us leave things at this. We shall meet again at least once more and decide from there. I'd like to get to know you better, but if ye doona wish it, I'll respect that."

"I'm good with that." He smiled. An answering smile formed on her face just before she and the Morrigan vanished in a spray of magic so bright, he shielded his eyes with a hand.

Jonathan covered the distance to Britta and Tarika. "I'll take you up on your offer for information too," he said to Britta. "There's so much I don't know."

"Ask away." Britta grinned. "Thank the goddess we're all together again."

"I'm grateful for that too." A corner of his mouth turned down. "Looks like I added a mother to the package. It's going to take a bit of maneuvering before I know how I feel about that. I hated her for a long time for abandoning Da and me…"

"Aye, but ye're going to give her a chance. I see it in your mind." Tarika puffed smoke skyward.

"Maybe. At least, I'm going to try."

Jonathan drew Britta into a quick embrace, marveling at the way her body fit perfectly with his, before they joined Tarika on her back.

"'Tis looking as if we'll have time for everything we need," Britta said from their perch atop the dragon. "I canna imagine the Celts brushing their problems aside. Not with the evidence Arianrhod presents against the Morrigan."

"Och, and I certainly can." Tarika huffed fire and flapped them toward the time-travel gateway.

Jonathan wrapped his arms around Britta. She pressed her body back against his and moved a hand behind her to cup his ridged flesh. No one was more surprised than he when he came alive under her touch. He buried his face in her hair and laughed because she felt so incredible in his arms.

"Are the two of you ready?" Tarika inquired. The words were pointed, but a fond undercurrent ran beneath them as she brought them down next to where the time portal had disgorged them.

"Aye," Britta said. "More than ready. Let us leave this place."

CHAPTER 16

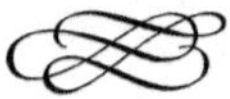

Britta sprawled on Mauvreen's broad front porch, leaning against Jonathan. They'd burned up more than a day in Earth's barren future. It was nearing eleven o'clock at night, and the sun had just set. She felt weary, yet deeply pleased because they'd won a significant battle. Even if the Morrigan managed to wrest a pardon from the Celts, it would take her years to find, and then train, other humans to do her bidding. The chances of her co-opting dragon shifters again was slim. Britta plucked another piece of crisp bread—Mauvreen called it a cracker—off a plate. She put a bit of cheese on it and ate hungrily.

The dragons lay on their bellies in the witch's yard as close to the house as they could get. Britta moved to a lower porch step so she could place her hand on Tarika's neck and held her cup out to Mary Elma, who was passing out more liquor. They'd spent most of the hour or so since they arrived filling the witches in on what transpired.

"I don't like it that the Morrigan is still on the loose." Mary Elma made a sour face. "Arianrhod being with her makes it a little better, but not much."

"Aye," Lachlan concurred. "And she is likely to remain *loose* from

176

the looks of things. I canna see the Celts doing more than slapping her hand and telling her to try to behave better."

"We doona know for certain," Tarika said. "Though I suspect ye're likely correct."

"Aye," Kheladin concurred. "Doona paint the devil on the wall, yet we shouldna be surprised if he surfaces."

Lachlan grinned. He trotted down the steps and sat next to his dragon. "Guess we'll just have to wait till one of the Celts shows up and we can grill him—or her."

"It may not help," Mary Elma said. "They're notoriously close-mouthed about things. And this is something they would consider delicate."

Mauvreen snorted. "You mean classified. Sort of a… 'We'll tell you, but then we'll have to kill you,' deal."

Britta nodded thoughtfully. "Ye're likely correct. They would deem it a Celtic god affair, not to be shared outside their ranks."

"Failing all else, I'll get Mother to tell me. Or try to, anyway." Jonathan drained his mug and handed it to Mary Elma. "Before we left, she told me she'd like to get to know me better."

Britta squealed as delight raced through her. "Not that I was exactly listening in, but I did hear her say that. Ye must be thrilled."

Jonathan shrugged. "Maybe *thrilled* is too big a word, but I am cautiously optimistic. Curious too. I really would like to learn more about her. Who knows? Maybe she could shed some light on Da. She said she would—before the Morrigan piped up with her two cents' worth." He shifted his position and stared at Mauvreen. "You were there. What did the Celts want with Da?"

The witch studied her hands before meeting his gaze. "I know— at least some of it—but I'm not sure it's my place to tell you. They leveraged his seer talents to augment their particular needs, but I'm sure you figured that part out on your own. The piece you're missing is why Angus allowed it." She pressed her lips together. "If Arianrhod won't fill you in, ask me again, and I will."

"Wise." Mary Elma nodded at her friend. "There's enough love lost between witches and Celts as things stand. No reason to add to the many things they hold against us."

Britta kept a close eye on Jonathan. He hadn't cared for Mauvreen's half-answer, but he had the good grace to remain silent. She squeezed his hand, and he tightened his in return.

"Before I get sidetracked, how does this time travel thing work?" Maggie glanced at her grandmother. "Those two children whose lives I saved, will the raw material to create them survive across the next half century?"

Mary Elma and Mauvreen exchanged glances. Jonathan leaned forward. Apparently, he was just as interested as Maggie in their answer. Britta was intrigued to hear the witches' explanation too. She had her own ideas and wondered if they'd jive with whatever Mary Elma and Mauvreen were about to share.

"You always did have a knack for asking hard questions." Mary Elma sighed.

"People have been trying to understand time travel forever," Mauvreen cut in. "Just look at all those movies, books, and television shows."

Maggie made a come along gesture with both hands. "I'm tired, Gran. The simplest explanation—if there is one—will satisfy me."

Mary Elma took a deep breath. "The *Star Trek* version of time travel where you can't move so much as a speck of dust and not end up with a domino effect isn't true. I can't be certain, but from the sound of what you told us, it's unlikely those same two children will be born when the primary timeline—the one we live in—moves forward."

"Why not?" Jonathan asked.

Mary Elma drew her arched, black brows together. "It's my fond hope that the work you did today means the forty years of war never happens. If it doesn't, humans won't be forced into living in caves like animals."

"I sort of understand," Maggie said. "Whatever circumstances drove those children's parents together likely won't exist. So their mom and dad may well marry other people and have children with them instead."

"Close enough," Mary Elma murmured.

"Were the children brother and sister, then?" Kheladin asked. Maggie nodded. "May I add to what ye said?" The dragon inclined his head toward Mary Elma.

"Please." A smile softened her usually austere features.

"The dragon understanding of time is somewhat different," Kheladin began. "There are infinite strands of time. The one we visited will continue to its logical conclusion."

"Do ye mean until Earth simply dies?" Lachlan asked.

"Aye, but if it isna a primary thread, it can fade without disrupting the main time bands where most of Earth's inhabitants live." Kheladin took a breath and exhaled steam. "Consider this. If ye returned to the fifteen hundreds, as Lachlan and I did, ye would find just what we found. Our life uninterrupted, where we could visit Lachlan's castle and hobnob with his kinsmen and with dragons I've known for centuries. That life is still there. As are other lives if we'd traveled back to the sixteen or seventeen hundreds."

"So if you've lived for hundreds of years—or thousands." Maggie looked pointedly at Tarika. "You can travel up or down the time continuum and tap into one of your previous lives, or a future one."

"'Tis a bit of a simplification," Tarika said. "But close enough."

"Fascinating," Jonathan murmured.

When Britta looked at him, his eyes shone with wonder, and her heart swelled with love. Despite how unfamiliar everything was to him, he'd risen to the challenge with enthusiasm and grace.

She focused her mind voice only for Tarika. *"Would ye mind if we left for a bit?"*

The dragon trumpeted so loudly, Britta half expected the people she saw walking past Mauvreen's house to come running. Then she remembered the warding and knew the strolling singles and couples couldn't see either them or Mauvreen's actual house. If they looked their way at all, passersby would see only a humble, white cottage with rose bushes planted in front.

Tarika snorted steam. "Kheladin and I made a wager on how long it would take you to ask. And if ye'd be the first or Lachlan."

"Ask what?" Jonathan draped an arm around Britta's shoulders.

She felt her face heat. "I told Tarika that ye and I might leave for a bit."

"Brilliant." He leapt to his feet and drew her upright. "What are we waiting for?"

"Maybe to tell your loved ones good-bye?" Mauvreen joined them. "And to plan when we'll meet next."

"I won." Kheladin's jaws opened, exposing double rows of razor sharp teeth.

Britta looked from one dragon to the other. "Before we go, which of you bet on whom?"

"Simple enough." Kheladin's eyes whirled faster. "I bet ye'd be the first to leave, and ye'd do so afore the middle of the night. Tarika bet on Lachlan."

"Is that so?" Britta put her hands on her hips. "So ye deduced my flesh would be weaker than his?"

Kheladin rolled his shoulders, making his scales clank. "Turns out I was right."

Jonathan laughed. It was infectious. Britta found it impossible to be angry with the dragons. "Next time," she patted Tarika's side, "bet on me, eh? Your verra own dragon shifter."

"I'll consider it...bondmate." The dragon winked.

Mary Elma upended the bottle of scotch. After drinking, she set it on the porch with a *clunk*. "All four of you could use a few days without the likes of us. It's Wednesday. Let's find one another at the Callanish Stones on Sunday at sunset. They're fascinating, and I'd like to spend more time there."

"In the meantime," Mauvreen gazed fondly at the dragons, "maybe we could trade witch knowledge for dragon lore."

"'Twould take far more than a few days," Tarika said, blowing smoke skyward.

"Well, we'll do the best we can." Mary Elma smiled warmly. She turned toward Maggie, Lachlan, Jonathan, and Britta. "Off with the bunch of you now. Try to get past the first blush of your obsession with one another, so we can concentrate on the next part when we regroup."

"What might that be?" Maggie asked, eying her grandmother.

"Why getting rid of the Morrigan once and for all. Mauvreen and I have been talking. We have some ideas if the Celts don't come through, but I'm sure our dragon friends will add to them."

Maggie snorted. "I know that look, Gran. Your eyes are actually twinkling."

"I'm sure I have no idea what you mean, my dear."

Britta walked into Jonathan's open arms and said, "We can leave now, afore the conversation gets any thicker."

"Grand idea."

She tapped into magic to return them to his house.

JONATHAN'S ARMS were still around Britta as his living room formed around them. He lowered his head and kissed her. She opened her mouth to his questing tongue, licking, nibbling, sucking. His cock hardened and pressed uncomfortably against the front of his trousers. He ran his hands down her backside and drew her as close to his body as he could. She bucked her hips against him and moaned low in her throat. He felt the points of her nipples pebble against his chest.

He broke their kiss and looked at her. At first her eyes were closed, but they fluttered open, and her amazing golden gaze snared him. "You're so beautiful." He moved a hand from her backside and smoothed hair away from her face.

"So are you." She ran her tongue down the side of his face and snaked it around the bottom of his ear. Hot and cold shivers cascaded through his body. "I was verra proud of you today."

"But I didn't do much of anything," he protested, still unable to tear his gaze from the perfection of her face.

"Och, but ye did. Ye have good instincts. 'Twas ye who first noticed the Morrigan helping Preki when he fought Kheladin." She paused for a beat. "And ye moved beyond your welter of confused feelings about Arianrhod pretty damned fast."

He shrugged, feeling self-conscious. "Blood calls to blood, I guess. Once I got partway over being angry with her, there wasn't much standing in the way." He traced the line of her jaw with a finger. "I don't want to talk about her. I want to talk about us. You were brave today too. You charged into the fray without a moment's hesitation."

"Aye, but I was born to combat, and I've had years to hone my skills with Tarika." She swallowed hard and drew back a little. "I'm not ashamed to tell you, I was frightened for my dragon. Once I knew she was shackled with iron, it turned my verra blood to ice. I've always seen her as invincible. That she'd been captured shook me to my core."

"They told us how they were taken by surprise and overpowered." Jonathan sucked in a breath. The dragons' story of what happened on South Uist Island had been hard to listen to. They'd fought valiantly, but it wasn't enough to save them.

Britta nodded. "It shocked me how easily the Morrigan masterminded their kidnapping."

He cupped the side of her face with his hand. "You'd have done anything to save Tarika. I saw it in your mind, in your face, in the set of your body."

She nodded. "Aye, I would've."

"Good." He brushed his knuckles over her lips. "Then you'll understand that's just the way I feel about you. I love you, Britta. I'd die to protect you."

She laid a finger over his lips. "Let us hope it doesna come to that because Tarika and I would fight to the death for you as well. She and I both love you."

He bit back an awkward laugh. "Here I'd planned to sweep you off your feet, make love with you, and we're talking about death and dying."

"Nay. We're talking of love. I love you, Jonathan James Shea, and I'm so grateful ye're a part of my life. Death. Battles. Sex. Life. 'Tis all intertwined. We doona get the sweet without the bitter. The joy without the pain."

He tightened his arms around her and stood just holding her, reveling in the feel of her body in his arms. "Would you like to bathe before we make love?"

"Aye." Her voice was muffled against his neck. "That would be nice, particularly since we doona have to scare up a servant to heat the water."

"May I undress you?" Jonathan's voice cracked. He felt suddenly shy. Though they'd made love before, this time words of love stood between them. He hoped his lovemaking would live up to their newly acknowledged feelings.

She stepped back from his embrace and nodded, her expression serious, her eyes shining with emotion. With his fingers suddenly none too steady, he slid her jacket off her shoulders and her top over her head. He reached behind her and unhooked the bra she'd borrowed from Maggie, dropping it atop her other clothes. His throat constricted; his heart thudded inside his chest.

"Your breasts are incredible." He traced the nipples with a fingertip.

She made a tight, little noise deep in her throat. "If ye keep that up, we willna get to the hot water. And I would like to bathe. I can smell myself."

He undid the fastenings of her pants and hoisted her until she sat atop an occasional table. Then he knelt to remove her shoes and socks. He caressed her feet with his hands, massaging the arches and each toe. She pushed them against him and sighed. "Och, but 'tis heavenly. Ye can rub my feet anytime ye want."

"Here." He rose and placed his hands on either side of her waist so he could lift her to her feet. A small push, and her pants slid to the floor, followed by her underwear. She stepped out of both.

"Are ye planning to bathe with all your clothes on?" she inquired impishly.

"Probably not a bad idea." He grinned. "They smell just about as bad as I do. We'll have to toss everything in the washer tomorrow."

"Another word I doona know." She reached for him and began removing his clothes. When she was done and he stood naked before her, cock jutting in front of him, she walked behind him and unbraided his hair. "Ye have the most amazing hair." She ran her fingers through it. "Long, thick, shiny. Any woman would be envious."

"Not you." He turned to face her. "Your hair is a miracle. I can't wait to see what our children will look like."

A soft smile wreathed her face. "I canna wait, either. Just as soon as we're certain there's no more danger…" A shadow crossed her features.

He shook his head and placed a hand on each of her shoulders. "You have nothing to worry about. I'll protect you. Care for you always. I set wards when we first entered my home. You can add to them if it makes you feel better. Tonight, there's just you and me, Britta, and our love for each other." He took her hand and led her down the hall to the bathroom. The tile felt cool beneath his feet as he bent to start the tub filling.

While they waited, he held her in his arms and rocked her against him. Sexual heat washed over him, receded, and built again. Knowing he would bury himself in her body before they slept was like a balm, a promise of their commitment to one another. "Tub's full enough," he murmured against her hair. "Why don't you get in?"

"What about you?"

He nuzzled her neck, tasting the sweetness of her skin, inhaling the scents that were hers, and hers alone. "I'll be right behind you. I just want to get a dipper so I can rinse the soap out of your hair."

He felt aroused but playful too. For the first time since he'd met Britta, it didn't feel as if the world would implode if he didn't get his cock inside her immediately. He lowered himself into the tub behind her, and she settled against his body. Tenderness for the woman in his arms filled him. Sandwiched between them, his cock twitched against her back. She arched and pressed against him.

"Ye feel exquisite."

"Nay, lassie." He aped her brogue. "Ye wrote the book on that one."

He worked soap into her skin and hair and rinsed her. She twisted in his arms and washed him, all except for his hair, which she couldn't reach. In the end, he slid down, dunked his head under, and soaped it. Britta stepped from the tub and helped him sluice water over his head until it ran clear.

She wrapped herself in a towel and held one out for him. He glanced at the water, wrinkled his nose, and stepped from the tub. "Wow! Pretty dingy. We probably should've let it out midway and run new."

"It doesna matter. We can bathe again come the morning. 'Tisn't far away. Summer nights are short this far north." She rubbed him dry, then turned to him and winked. "No more excuses. We're clean, fed, the only thing left—"

"—is to tell you you're the most beautiful woman in the entire world. And I'm the luckiest man." His breath caught in his throat, and he crushed her against him. No more waiting. He'd toyed with his passion for hours. He closed his mouth over hers, feeling her open to him. Her tongue sparred with his. He pushed the towels trapped between them aside, desperate to feel her skin against his.

She wrapped her arms around him and buried her hands in his wet hair, her mouth still glued to his. Her nipples hardened where they pressed against his chest, and she made a little moaning noise he'd come to recognize. The lust he'd denied roared to life. He ran his hands down her back. She had the silkiest skin. Her scent intensified, along with her passion. He inhaled lavender, amber, and the musk of her arousal.

He raised his mouth from hers and strung kisses down her neck, bending to capture a nipple in his mouth. She gasped and pulled him against her. He moved from one nipple to the other, lost in the wonder of her body. Kneeling, he moved his mouth lower and settled between her legs, licking and sucking her sensitive nub cradled in its nest of red-gold curls.

Britta thrust her pelvis against him. Her legs shook where he leaned his head against her thighs. "Hurry," she murmured. "Och, hurry. I canna stand much more."

Jonathan cast a glance at the towel-strewn bathroom floor but opted for the bed. His cock felt like it would burst anyway, no matter what happened next. He rose to his feet and scooped her into his arms. Carrying her across the hall, he placed her tenderly atop his bed.

She lay in the welter of bedclothes left from their last lovemaking and kindled a mage light. Her skin took on a golden hue in its glow. Surrounded by her long, damp hair, she looked like a goddess. A Botticelli angel.

"What would you like, my love?"

"Ye. Inside me. Now."

"I could put my mouth back on you," he teased. It wasn't easy to talk. His balls ached. His cock was on fire.

She rolled into a sit and wrapped her hands around his shaft. Her mouth followed. The heat of her was almost more than he could tolerate. When she circled his glans with her tongue, he cried out.

"Och." She kept her hands on him but tilted her head back. "Did I hurt you?"

"No. Everything gets really sensitive when I'm about to come."

She moved her hands to his hips and pulled him onto the bed. Flashing a coquettish smile, she turned away and got onto her hands and knees. The view of her pussy with its halo of tight curls drove everything else from his mind. He wrapped a hand around his cock and guided it into her. He tried to not move, to make the moment last, but she tightened her muscles around him, tentative at first, and then again and again. He moved a hand between her legs and gripped her hip with the other. Sensation built until he couldn't hold back any longer and plunged into her.

He wanted her, needed her, had to claim her for his own. His penis developed a mind of its own, and he followed its lead, plumbing her until there was nothing in the world but the silky, scorching heat of her around his shaft and the delicious sensations turning his entire body into an enchanted lightning rod.

She came, screaming her ecstasy. He kept rubbing her clit as he slammed into her. Maybe, just maybe, he could hold off long enough for her to come a second time. His cock had never been so hard. Awareness poured through him. Of her, of him, of the magic they created together. Rhythmic contractions began high in her vault, and he knew she was coming again. He let go of any semblance of control.

His climax began deep in his belly, and his balls snugged against his body. Semen raced from him in huge spasms that shook him to his core. He heard himself cry out and then say her name over and over like a wish or a prayer.

Stunned by the passion that had passed between them, it was all Jonathan could do to guide them to where they lay next to one another. He turned her toward him and placed a hand on either side of her face. "I love you. God, but I love you." Emotion was so close to the surface, he felt raw, exposed. But he had nothing to hide from this woman.

"Aye." She smiled, soft, tender, and brushed her lips over his. "I love you too. We shall be together throughout time, ye and I."

"Promise?"

"Promise. No matter what befalls us. We are joined, body and soul." Britta grinned. "And dragon. Doona forget about her. She was with us just now, in my mind. She's happy for us."

Doubts that had plagued him, silly qualms about work and where they'd live and how they'd manage, fell away. All that mattered was right here in his arms. "Tell her thank you."

"Tell her yourself," Tarika's voice echoed in his head.

"My heart's so full, I scarcely know where to begin." Jonathan shut his eyes for a moment to focus his thoughts. When he opened them, he knew the best thing would be to keep it simple. *"Thank you for sharing your life with me. I'm most humbly grateful and I'll do everything I can to be worthy of both of you."*

"Ye picked well," Tarika told Britta.

"Aye, I know. See you verra soon, bondmate."

"The Callanish stones four days hence."

"We shall be there," Britta concurred.

Her mage light moved closer and dimmed. She ran her hands down his face and shoulders. "Sleep, my love. Tarika and I will take first watch."

He felt her spell but didn't fight it as his eyelids grew heavy. "Wake me so you get some sleep too."

"Aye, I will. I doona need much rest."

Cradled against her body, Jonathan slid toward sleep. His last conscious thoughts were of riding astride Tarika with Britta in front of him and the wind whipping against his face.

Dragons, magic, shifters, goddesses. I was born for this.

"Aye, love, that ye were. And we'll challenge your magic to its utmost, but not until tomorrow—at the earliest." The sweet chimes of Britta's laughter lulled him to sleep.

*A*rianrhod moved briskly up steps leading to the Celtic gods' main meeting room in Inverlochy Castle on the south bank of the River Lochy. To human eyes, it lay in ruins, but magic could resurrect most anything. The Morrigan pranced along by her side in the form of a teenaged girl, blonde curls bouncing, silken skirts rustling against the wooden risers. Arianrhod blew out a tense breath. The Morrigan hadn't given her a whit of trouble, but Arianrhod was drained from keeping her guard up. She'd been ready for anything, from an outright attack to the Morrigan pulling power and making a run for it, but the only thing the Battle Crow did was don her current form a few minutes ago.

Arianrhod had called the other Celts telepathically. While they might not all be here to meet her and the Battle Crow, at least some of them would. She hoped. She was on fairly shaky ground after the revelation about her true-born, half-Druid son.

If I'm verra lucky, the others willna hold it against me. After all, 'twas many years ago.

She glared at the Morrigan. "Why'd ye pick a maid's illusion?"

The Morrigan shrugged. For a moment, the expression on her

face was anything but what a fifteen-year-old innocent would wear. Understanding dawned.

"I get it." Arianrhod grunted. "Ye think if ye appear childlike, virginal yet slightly slutty, 'twill go easier with you."

"Well." The Morrigan licked her lips suggestively. "They are mostly men."

And easily sidetracked.

"If ye're verra skilled," Arianrhod didn't bother to temper her sarcasm, "mayhap ye can get a battle going in our council chamber."

"Oooh, splendid suggestion. Doona tempt me."

Arianrhod pulled open the twelve-foot high oaken door. "Get in there," she commanded and followed the Battle Crow into a huge chamber decorated with crystals and natural stone in every hue of the rainbow. Rich carpets covered the stone floors, thick wool woven with depictions of Celtic glory. A fire burned in an enormous hearth that took up one end of the room. Ceridwen sat before the fire stirring her cauldron. A handful of other Celts looked up from where they sat.

"Sister." Gwydion got slowly to his feet. "What have we here?"

Arianrhod gave the Morrigan a push. "Get yourself to the witness seat. Ye've been trouble enough."

"As ye say, mistress." The lovely girl-woman that was the Morrigan dropped a curtsey and sashayed up the center aisle, her hips swaying provocatively. She pushed her blonde curls over her shoulders and settled onto a plain, oak chair on a raised dais.

"What we have here," Arianrhod strode to her brother's side, "is the Morrigan."

"Aye." He nodded tiredly. "I can see through her illusion, but why have ye directed her to the tribunal seat?"

"Let's do this formally." Arianrhod swept past him and up to the front of the room. She turned and faced the Celtic gods, disappointed so few had heeded her call. "I found the Morrigan in a future time. She'd kidnapped two dragons and had them chained to a tower with iron."

A collective gasp spread through the room. Andraste, goddess of victory, surged to her feet and shook her blonde hair out of her face. "Is this true?" she demanded.

"Och." The maid masquerading as the Morrigan cast her eyes downward. "I am afraid it is. I doona know quite what came over me, but when Arianrhod pointed out the error of my ways, I freed the dragons immediately. And I also helped do away with two dragon shifters, who'd actually chained the dragons to that tower."

"Two dragon shifters ye'd co-opted to do your bidding hundreds of years ago," Arianrhod inserted smoothly.

"It scarcely matters." The Morrigan's voice was sweet, melodic, and laced with compulsion. "They are dead and their dragons' souls safely ensconced in Fire Mountain. 'Twas a decent ending, if ye ask me."

Ceridwen rose from her place next to her cauldron. She stalked in front of the Morrigan. "Enough shenanigans. Take one of your common forms. I doona wish to look upon this new creation of yours."

"As ye will." The maid shimmered, and the Battle Crow took form where she'd sat. "There." The crow cocked her head to one side. "Am I more…acceptable as a bird?"

Ceridwen turned to face her fellow Celts. "The Morrigan admits she broke the covenant betwixt us and the dragons. What shall her punishment be?"

Arianrhod took a deep breath and raked her tired eyes over the small group. While she was grateful for Ceridwen's assistance, she had a hard time believing the Morrigan would suffer at all for what she'd done.

We're not good at meting out punishment to our own.

Andraste stepped forward. "Found any good battles lately, crow?"

The Morrigan cawed. "Nay. 'Tis part of the problem. I grew bored and sought to entertain myself."

Something in Arianrhod snapped. "Mayhap, afore you pass

judgment," she said to the Celts, "you should travel into the future. Not far. Fifty years will do. Take a good, hard look at a dying planet. All that is the Morrigan's doing. What she isna saying is that Lachlan, a dragon shifter, found the woman prophesied to stand by his side and defeat the Crow. All her maneuvering has been to prevent it from happening. First, she targeted Lachlan—ensorcelling him for over three hundred years—then Lachlan's woman, and finally, his dragon."

Arianrhod paused to take a measured breath. "Lachlan's woman is granddaughter to Mary Elma Hibbins, the most powerful witch—"

"Aye, I know well enough who she is," Ceridwen spoke over her. "It appears we need more information." Ceridwen folded her hands in front of her.

"Aye." Andraste nodded. "I agree."

"Fine." Arawn stepped forward. "We shall reconvene in one week's time."

"What would you have me do between now and then?" the Morrigan asked in honeyed tones.

"Whatever ye would," Arawn replied. "We have no way to imprison you."

"Aye, and we can find you if ye doona return." Andraste turned her agate green eyes on the Morrigan.

"Och aye, and then I'm free to leave?" The crow took an anticipatory step forward.

Ceridwen made shooing motions with both hands. "Please. I prefer the air in this room without ye in it."

Incredulous that all her hard work had been for naught, Arianrhod watched as the Morrigan drew power and vanished. She turned on her peers. "I canna believe—"

"Ye canna believe what?" Gwydion strode to her side. "We have no way to imprison her. We canna kill her."

"Ye could send her to Fire Mountain for the rest of time," Arianrhod sputtered.

"Only if the dragons agreed." Her brother sounded annoyed to be bothered. "'Tis enough for one day. We shall see how we are feeling a week from now."

Arianrhod plodded toward the end of the chamber, so dispirited all she wanted to do was find her bed and sleep for days. Tense from riding herd on the Morrigan—and for nothing, it appeared—every bone and muscle in her body complained. She hadn't expected much, but this was far less than even her most pessimistic imaginings.

"Sister." Gwydion's voice stopped her.

She didn't turn around. "Aye."

"I would talk with you further about your half-Druid son."

"Later, brother. Much later."

Filled with sudden purpose that infused needed energy into her aching bones, Arianrhod summoned power and was gone. She had to warn Jonathan and his dragon shifter consort. Lachlan and Kheladin too. And the witches. They had no idea the Morrigan was still on the loose. As she traveled, her thoughts took form. Maybe she'd stay with Jonathan and Britta for a span of days—if they'd have her. Just long enough to teach Jonathan more about his magic and to protect them in case the Morrigan, swept up by a need for revenge, decided to call.

Aye, mayhap I can tell him about his father and me. What he knows now makes him pity Angus. And despise me.

She set her mouth in a harsh line as the truth of her thoughts sank in.

Arianrhod considered redirecting her traveling spell, then thought better of it. Now that her secret was out, there was no reason she and Angus couldn't make a life together, but she'd have to ferret him out from wherever he'd sequestered himself to let him know.

If he still wanted her.

It seemed likely, but in truth she had no idea.

If she went after Angus right now, though, it would offer the

Morrigan far too much latitude to wreak havoc. Nay, her first plan was best. After she let everyone know the Battle Crow was still in the game, she could hunt for Angus. The thought of seeing him again after all this time made her heart glad. She'd kept to herself in the years since turning their son over to him to care for and never taken another lover.

Weariness fell away as she materialized in an older section of Inverness near Jonathan's energy. She took care to cloak herself in invisibility until she was certain no one would see her simply pop out of nowhere. Mortals scared easily, and she didn't need the complication of a screeching human just now.

Despite not having an address, finding her flesh and blood was a simple enough matter, and she zeroed in on an eighteenth century structure, built of stone and stout timbers.

For the first time in a long time, she had something to look forward to, and a smile split her face as she made her way into the building where her son lived.

You've reached the end of *Dragon Maid*. Please take a moment to leave a review.
This series is completed in *Dragon's Dare*, Dragon Lore, Book Four.
Read on for a sample of *Dragon's Dare*.

ABOUT THE AUTHOR

Ann Gimpel is a USA Today bestselling author. A lifelong aficionado of the unusual, she began writing speculative fiction a few years ago. Since then her short fiction has appeared in a number of webzines and anthologies. Her longer books run the gamut from urban fantasy to paranormal romance. Once upon a time, she nurtured clients, now she nurtures dark, gritty fantasy stories that push hard against reality. When she's not writing, she's in the backcountry getting down and dirty with her camera. She's published over 70 books to date, with several more planned for 2019 and beyond. A husband, grown children, grandchildren and wolf hybrids round out her family.

Keep up with her at www.anngimpel.com or http://anngimpel.blogspot.com

If you enjoyed what you read, get in line for special offers and pre-release special reads. Sign up for Ann's newsletter on her website or her blog.

DRAGON LORE, BOOK FOUR

Jonathan Shea cradled Britta in his arms. She was asleep, the rhythm and cadence of her breathing revealed her exhaustion. He still couldn't believe he'd found a mate, and a woman linked to a dragon at that. Britta KilKerran was actually the Countess of Cumbria, or she had been a few hundred years back. He wasn't certain such a title still existed.

It didn't matter. What did was he'd offer up his life to protect the woman slumbering against his chest. He loved her dragon too, but Tarika scarcely needed his protection. When he thought of the scarlet-scaled dragon, one of the First Born, the place on his neck where she'd marked him with a mating bite tingled. It was her contribution to his bond with Britta.

She stirred in his arms. He stroked strands of long, red-gold hair away from her face and spun a small spell to keep her asleep. They'd just come from a major battle to free Tarika and Kheladin, another dragon, from the Morrigan's clutches. Both of them needed rest, but his heart and mind were too full to let go quite yet.

After years of never believing the rumor about his mother being a Celtic deity, he'd finally met her. He brought it on himself by calling for her when they desperately needed help, but he never believed she'd actually show up. Regardless, he couldn't deny her existence anymore—no matter how much he might want to. Arianrhod had abandoned him when he was so young he had no memories of her, and when he cut to the bone of things, he resented the crap out of her neglect.

Jonathan shut his eyes for a moment and summoned an image of his father. Tall and rangy with shaggy rich brown hair and amber eyes, Angus had been a dreamer. He did his best for Jonathan, but often as not, he'd been caught up in some trance state or another. Though Angus hadn't said so, Jonathan understood his father was relieved when he grew old enough to be on his own. Once Jonathan left Ireland, Angus vanished. Their modest cabin near Inishowen remained, but Jonathan knew better than to waste time hunting for a man who didn't wish to be found.

Had Arianrhod seen Angus all these years he'd been missing? Jonathan could ask her, but she might just stare him down with those inscrutable eyes—one gold, the other silver—and not bother to answer.

He tightened his hold on Britta, and she nestled closer. She was more comfortable about Arianrhod being his mother than he was, but then she was far more comfortable with magic in general than him too. He blew out a breath, recognizing his life would never be the same.

Not that he wanted it to be, but he would've preferred finding the love of his life without having to deal with a long-lost parent. Particularly one who stirred up a welter of prickly feelings. Now if Angus were to show back up, it would be a different story…

Britta wriggled against him, and her golden eyes flickered open. She regarded him sleepily through thick red lashes. "Ye canna rest, my love?"

Jonathan shrugged and offered a sheepish smile. "Lots to think about."

She cupped the side of his face in one hand. "Do ye wish to talk about anything?"

He shrugged again, feeling uncomfortable. What was there to say, really? He was a little old to be struggling with parent issues, besides he'd long since come to terms with his father's magic being almost too strong to allow him to spend much time around normal humans. Jonathan dealt with some level of that as well, but his job as a software engineer who designed games let him keep to himself.

Britta brushed her hand across his lips. "Whenever ye wish, I'll be here. Tarika too. She's verra old and much wiser than either of us. If ye canna get the information elsewhere, mayhap we can figure out what sort of hold the Celtic gods had on your da."

"Thank you. I'll keep it in mind." Jonathan reached around her and snagged a bottle of Irish whiskey off the nightstand. "Would you like some? I can get us glasses."

"Och, and I can drink from the bottle. No need to get fancy." She smiled, and it transformed her into something so striking he couldn't look away. A high forehead gave way to sculpted cheekbones and a defined chin. One of his old T-shirts covered her from chest to knees, but the outline of her breasts was clearly visible through the well-aged beige fabric.

His cock stirred, and he rolled his eyes. "We made love twice after we got here. I don't understand why I can't get enough of you."

"Are ye complaining?" She quirked an arched red brow.

He shook his head and drew both of them to a half sitting position against the carved oak headboard. He uncorked the bottle and handed it to her. She drank deep before handing it back.

Britta narrowed her eyes and watched him drink. "We're far from home free," she blurted without preamble.

"Which problem are you referring to?" He placed the bottle on a side table without bothering to cork it. He wasn't done yet, and likely neither was Britta.

She moved away and sat cross-legged facing him, her lovely face creased with concern. "We may have permanently removed Connor and Rhukon and their dragons from the action, but there have to be other corrupt dragon shifters. We must seek them out and destroy them too."

Jonathan shook his head. "It won't matter unless we get to the heart of things."

"Aye, ye're correct. We must find a way to corral the Morrigan, or she'll just entice more mages and dragons with promises of limitless power." Britta caught her lower lip between her teeth. "Tarika plans to warn the dragons. She believes the dark mages want to drain their dragon bondmates' power."

Jonathan straightened and recaptured the whiskey bottle, taking another swallow. "I thought mages became dragon shifters because they loved dragons and wished to share their lives with them."

"Aye and that would be true—for most of us. Power lures dark mages, though. Far more power than can be had through the normal dragon shifter bond."

"How do you know?"

"I saw it in Connor and Rhukon's minds afore we thrashed them."

"You didn't say anything." He handed her the bottle. Maybe they should eat something, if they were going to drink much more.

"I would have. Eventually. Tarika and I needed to determine just what it meant. And if 'tis really true, or just conjecture on our part."

He kissed her forehead before swinging his legs over the side of the bed. "I'm going to cut up a bit of cheese for us and get some crackers." He pulled on a pair of black sweat pants, securing the waist string to keep them from falling down, and got to his feet.

"Excellent." She grinned. "Plotting revenge is hungry business, but ye dinna have to cover that amazing cock."

He bit back a laugh, enjoying the compliment, and made his way to the kitchen. His apartment was small enough to keep talking. "Did you discuss this with Lachlan?" he asked as he chopped cheese off a block and opened a box of biscuits.

"Nay, but Tarika and Kheladin figured out what was going on while they were held prisoner."

Jonathan returned to the bedroom and plopped the snacks on the bed next to Britta. "How does this bondmate thing work? Would Lachlan be privy to the dark mage problem, if it's in his dragon's mind?"

"Not necessarily." She put cheese on a cracker and munched it down. "Not that Lachlan couldna force truth from his dragon, but if he saw no reason to be heavy handed, Kheladin could maintain independent thoughts, particularly now that we can remain in our own skins."

Jonathan looked at the crackers, but took another slug of whiskey instead. "What do you think of being able to be separate from your dragon? Before Kheladin uncovered the ancient magic that altered your bond, your shared consciousness was linked to one form or the other."

"Eat something." She handed him a cracker piled with cheese and waited until he put it into his mouth. "I liked the new system well enough—until the Morrigan shanghaied my dragon. Then I dinna like it at all." Britta tossed her hands in front of her. "Overall, I suppose 'tis an improvement since we can leverage both our strengths at the same time."

He settled himself carefully on the bed and ate another cracker before leaning against the headboard. He really was hungry, and the whiskey buzzed through his head, adding an eldritch glow to things. "We should target the Morrigan first and then hunt for other corrupt mage-dragon duos."

Britta frowned. "And here I was thinking 'twould be simpler to identify the dark mages first."

"Simpler, yes, but not smart. Once you begin that process, it'll spur the Morrigan to further evil."

The line between Britta's eyebrows deepened. "Aye, ye're likely right. Must be those cunning, wee games ye design."

"*Cunning wee games* is it?" Jonathan aped her brogue and laughed. "Aye, lassie. If it's one thing designing computer games taught me, it's strategy."

"Ye'll need all that talent because the Morrigan is immortal."

"Yeah, just like my mother." Jonathan winced. Where the fuck had that come from?

"Mayhap your da too." Britta's voice was gentle. "From the feel of your energy, I'd bet on it." She paused a beat. "Was Arianrhod one of the reasons ye couldna sleep?"

He nodded reluctantly. "Who has a Celtic goddess for a mother?" When Britta opened her mouth, he hurried on. "Nah, don't answer that. I suppose I always knew the rumors were true, but she wasn't around, so I could ignore them."

"Dinna your da ever speak of her?"

"No. If I asked, he pulled magic that muddled my mind—made me forget what it was I wanted to know. After a time, I stopped asking. When I got older, witches in our coven looked askance at me, but Mauvreen kept them at bay."

Britta grinned. "I like her, and Maggie's grandmother, Mary Elma, too. Nothing quite like a strong witch to keep me on my toes."

Jonathan snorted. "Lachlan certainly treats Mary Elma with kid gloves, and if I'm any judge, that's far from normal for him."

Britta's grin widened. "Maggie's his mate. Of course he'd be respectful of her grandmother, but beyond that Lachlan's a different man than the one I knew in the sixteen hundreds and earlier. Less brash and headstrong. Losing over three hundred years to being ensorcelled would change anyone, though."

"No kidding. I meant to ask him about that experience, but there's never been time. Back to Mauvreen, she was like a mom to me, always around, making certain I had what I needed."

"Did she never have children of her own?"

"No. No men that I could see, either. Magic runs strong in her, and she devoted her life to honing her craft alongside Maggie's grandmother. Speaking of which, Mary Elma was going to rally the covens to help with whatever plan we hatch up."

Britta waggled a finger in front of his face. "Och, and ye'll not sidestep things so easily."

"Sidestep what?" He handed her the whiskey, knowing full well what she meant.

"Arianrhod takes some getting used to."

Defensiveness prickled at the back of his neck. "Any parent who abandoned you would."

"Och aye, but she isna just *any parent*. She's the virgin huntress, and having a child in tow would've been a wee bit challenging to explain."

"She should've thought of that before she—" He bit off the rest of his sentence. It sounded whiny and sanctimonious.

Britta moved the cracker plate to a side table and straddled his lap. Her golden gaze bored into him and she pried the whiskey bottle out of his hand, laying it aside, but not letting go of his hand. She pressed a breast into it, and he felt her nipple stiffen at the contact.

"What were ye thinking about when first we touched?" Her gaze never left his. "When first we kissed?"

His cock roared to life from the heat of her body sitting across his lap. Breath hitched in his throat, and he rubbed her nipple through the thin fabric separating his hand from her breast. "Not a fair question," he mumbled.

"Och, and why not?" She pressed into his hand and moved her fingers between them to curve around his rigid flesh. "Do ye believe we're the first to ever be so hungry for one another 'tis all we can think about?"

"You're talking about sex, but babies are different..." He sputtered and tried again. "They are things to prevent—"

She laid her other hand, the one not curled around his cock, across his mouth. "Ye doona know. Ye werena there, so ye canna judge."

Truth in her words shamed him, but his uneasiness faded fast as desire flashed through him, turning his nerves to molten heat. He fumbled with the string at his waist, eager to get to his cock. She was naked beneath his T-shirt, so he could slip inside her, feel the enchanted heat of her surround him.

She added her fingers to the task of untying his drawstring, and their hands bumped against one another. The sound of their breathing pounded against his ears.

"Gods, but I love you." He gave up on his pants long enough to trace her full lower lip with his thumb.

"Aye, laddie, I love you too." She squirmed, and warmth from her core seared him. Britta bent forward and closed her mouth over his. Her breath was sweet from the whiskey they'd shared, and her tongue snaked inside his mouth, dancing with his. He clasped her hips between his hands and dry thrust against her body, so impatient to penetrate her, blood thundered through his veins.

An alien sound intruded, but he couldn't make sense of it. Until he heard it again and froze.

Britta tore her mouth from his and straightened. Color rose from her neck to the top of her head, and she swiveled her body to face Arianrhod. "Ye dinna knock. Ye should've."

"Aye, but I did knock. And so many times one of the neighbors came out to see what the ruckus was." Arianrhod's unusual eyes—one gold, one silver—twinkled with amusement. She shrugged. "I knew you were here, so I waited until the neighbor thought I left, then let myself in."

Jonathan got his breathing under control. His cock would take longer, but Britta still straddled him, so she hid the worst of things.

"I apologize for what appears to be poor timing." Arianrhod turned away to offer them privacy. "I'll wait in the front room, but you must dress, and we must talk."

"Are we going somewhere?" Britta asked.

"Aye, traveling clothes would be appropriate. I should've been more specific." Arianrhod walked through the door leading to the small combination living room and kitchen, clad in battle leathers that fit her tall, lithe form like a second skin. Her silver hair was braided in many small sections, but it still hung to her knees.

"How'd you find us?" With a last, lingering caress, Jonathan moved Britta off him and got off the bed to hunt down something to wear.

"Ask something important." Arianrhod's voice floated back to him, and he felt like an idiot. Of course the moon mother goddess, who controlled the tides and was also the virgin huntress, could manage something as simple as locating one with her own blood. For Christ's sake, even he could've accomplished something like that.

"'Tis on account of most of his blood not being in his brain at the moment," Britta trilled, followed by a burst of laughter. Arianrhod joined in, adding peals of mirth to Britta's.

"If the two of you plan on male bashing, forget it." He swatted Britta's ass, as she bent to work her legs into leather breeches not unlike Arianrhod's.

Jonathan donned dark wool trousers and a black turtleneck. He tossed a plaid lumberman's jacket over one arm and made his way toward the living room. As an afterthought, he doubled back for the whiskey.

Arianrhod hunkered before one of the many bookshelves lining the room, looking through its contents. She straightened and turned to face him. "Eclectic," she murmured.

"Glad you approve," he said stiffly.

"Och, and ye're not happy with me sifting through your things."

She hadn't posed it as a question, so he said, "That's right. Tell me what was so important you had to break into my home."

She drew her silver brows together. "A wee bit harsh, but true enough. Will ye sit?"

"No, I'd rather stand."

Britta walked in from the bedroom, brush in hand, and perched on the edge of an easy chair. Once there, she worked on her long hair, untangling and braiding it out of the way. "Doona mind me." She sent half a smile skittering across the room, aimed for Arianrhod.

The goddess twisted his straight-backed computer chair so it faced the center of the room and sat. "Ye are both in danger," she said without preamble. "The Celts dinna censure the Morrigan—"

"What?" Britta screeched. "Why ever not? Surely they recognized her culpability."

Arianrhod rolled her eyes. "Aye, of course they did. They are far from stupid, but flawed as the Battle Crow is, she's one of them."

"I doona understand." Britta's voice returned to its usual, musical cadence. "Dragons punish their own, why not Celts?"

"We never have."

"If that's true," Jonathan broke in, "why did you expect they'd react differently this time? It took a lot of effort to drag that bitch in front of the Celtic Council."

"Because the Morrigan broke the compact between us and dragons by kidnapping dragons and by plotting to siphon dragon magic through the corrupt dragon shifter bond."

"How do ye know that last?" Britta demanded. "'Tis what I suspect, yet we never talked of it, and neither Tarika nor I know for sure."

"Same way ye do, Missy." Arianrhod's voice cracked from weariness, or emotion, Jonathan couldn't tell. "I read it from the minds of the dragon shifters we killed."

"Did ye mention that to the other gods?" Britta asked.

"I dinna get a chance."

Britta tossed a cloak across her shoulders and linked an arm through Jonathan's. "We must leave. Now. The Celtic Council will answer to me for their disgraceful inattention to duty."

Arianrhod shot to her feet. "Not yet." Power spilled from her in waves, and it was all Jonathan could do to not step back a few paces. "I told you we must talk, and talk we shall. Corrupt dragon shifter mages are far from new. That's who ensorcelled Lachlan and Kheladin hundreds of years back. Multiple tasks lay afore us, and we must sort how to attack them."

The goddess' power snaked around Jonathan, and she walked

until she was nose to nose with him. "Unfinished business simmers between us. I would deal with it afore aught else."

Jonathan squared his shoulders. "It's not necessary—"

"Aye, but 'tis." She spoke over him. "Sit or stand. I doona care, but what ye will do is listen."

"Would ye like me to shield myself so I canna hear?" Britta asked.

Arianrhod sent an appraising glance her way. "Nay. Ye're his mate. Ye need to hear this too. While ye're at it, invite your dragon to listen through the bond ye share."

www.ingramcontent.com/pod-product-compliance
Lightning Source LLC
Chambersburg PA
CBHW071258190726
48292CB00007B/2584